BIRD OF PASSAGE

Dr. Nooshie Motaref

Lauri Burke, Cover Illustration

A3D Impressions
Tucson | Minneapolis

Remember me when I'm only a memory

5

BIRD OF PASSAGE

Published by

A3D Impressions

P.O. Box 57415, Tucson, AZ 85735
www.a3dimpressions.com
a3dimpressions@gmail.com

Publisher's Cataloging-in-Publication data available

Paperback: 978-1-7371922-8-2
eBook: 978-1-7371922-9-9

Lauri Burke, cover illustration
Donn Poll, book design

In ancient Indo-European mythology, Mitra refers to a woman
"Truth speaking… with a thousand ears…
ten thousands eyes… full knowledge,
strong, sleepless, and ever awake. Mitra is also protector
and keeper of all aspects of interpersonal relationships
such as friendship and love."

—*Avesta*, Zoroastrian holy book

ACKNOWLEDGMENTS

My gratitude goes to many wonderful individuals whose encouragements and supports navigate me through my journey.

Lauri Burke, your quiet wisdom caused me loud enough to drown out other voices and pointed me toward my expressive path. I praise you for being my muse in the Western World. You are a skillful painter and have brought this front page into existence with your amazing artistic talent. This cover is a piece of art, and I'm proud that it covers my story. This delightful picture captures its essence well—the bird is flying to freedom.

Rick Wamer, Donn Poll, and Dina Delany, at A3D Impressions, LLC: I am thankful for these smart and hardworking professionals and command them once again. Their dedication, efforts, and commitment to publishing yet another outstanding work is much appreciated.

There are many book-loving people and friends who always surprise me with their moral support and friendship. Among them, Farah Boroomand who planted the seed for a sequel to *Tapestries of the Heart*. Elahe Amani, the President of Women's Intercultural Network (WIN), I admire you for the superb annual literary festival you organize. Glenda Bonin, and Ron Lancaster of Tucson Tellers of Tales, in coaching me with diligence toward the art of storytelling, thank you. Loydene Lazich, with your magic wand throughout the years, you've made the upheaval times much more tolerable for many, including me.

And giving a shout-out to my friends on Twitter, Facebook and LinkedIn for making life interesting.

To my loved ones, for putting up with me and motivating me, especially to my parents in heaven, who raised a free thinker. THANK YOU ALL!

1980

SWITZERLAND, an enchanting land. Heaven for tycoons. Hell for have nots. And a neutral country for the rest of us. This land has become a temporary haven for me, Mitra. My name had taken roots in a mythical Persian woman. As legends have it, Mitra's birth was at the end of the coldest and longest night of the year, the winter solstice. She was that first ray of sun to illuminate the world. According to my mother, Maman Iran, my birth also happened when the first sunbeam lit the dark sky.

At age 28, I grew up to know well that I have an imperfect look, compared to Maman, or my only sibling, five years younger than me, Layla, who has milky skin and almond-shaped eyes. My typical hawk nose like my father, Baba Nima's, with a dramatic arched shape and a protruding bridge opposes their snob noses, small in perfect length and slightly upturned.

Maman always encouraged me to have a nose job. But I was too chicken to listen to her and go under the knife. Or it might be because of Baba Nima's remark: "Dear Mitra, it doesn't matter how we look outside, it matters how we feel inside."

I was proud of my linage reaching far back to Ormazd and Amaya who lived six hundred years before the birth of Christ. My ancestors refused to immigrate from Persia to India at the time of Zoroastrians' persecution in the seventh century. Instead, they abided by the rule of the land and converted to Islam when conquered by the Arabs in order to prevent bloodshed.

This afternoon, I arrived in this extravagant land in search of a new visa. Otherwise, the thoughts of coming to this lavish realm never would've entered my mind. I was alone, unlike other well-to-do Persians leaving Iran with their immediate families. From my hotel room window at the Central Plaza Hotel in the heart of Zurich, the outside scenery soothed me. The red clouds were announcing the departure of the sun. Everything appeared quiet despite some dark patches of clouds on the far horizon. I refused to consider my obscure future, regardless of my clenched hands and painful jaws.

It used to be we grabbed our passports and set out throughout Europe, Asia, and Africa. And if we were super-duper-rich, or connected to the royal family, even getting the American visa would be as easy as drinking a glass of water. However, not anymore. All this because some overzealous Iranian students took over the American embassy in Tehran and held a few Americans hostage in November 1979. Ever since, not only my life went upside down, but the entire world turned against my nation. As if the sky fell onto our heads.

Breaking away from the dictatorship regime of Khomeini made me smile. He brought chaos and instability to our lives by forcing us to follow Sharia's law, which some Iranians, including my family, had not known. To believe that it was beneath the true Islam, humanity, and Mohammad's instructions.

I breathed easier in this Western country, even though this was not my homeland. Only one month ago, Baba Nima announced, "Mitra! Don't be too hopeful of getting your exit visa out of Iran."

"Why not?" I asked, quite surprised.

"Now, the clergies are in charge, and no one travels anywhere, especially out of Iran. To see a single, young woman with so many stamps in her passport from Europe to America, makes them suspicious of her motive."

His comments baffled me. "Is it against the law too for a woman to travel to Switzerland as a tourist?"

"Thank God!" Maman Iran chimed in. "If you had a husband, then you'd have to get your husband's permission too."

I looked into her sad eyes. "I'm so blessed. I still have my freedom without submitting to any man." I paused. "Remember the time when I called from America asking for your thoughts on marrying a Persian man?"

"Ali!" Maman's face lit up.

Baba scratched his head. "No! What was that all about?"

To refresh their memories, I said, "I met him while I was doing my research at the Library of Congress. I'd thought he was a Moslem because of his name."

"Ah, yes," my father jogged his memory, "to tell us he converted to Christianity, even though his family was Moslem."

"In Islam," Maman Iran said, "a Moslem woman marrying a non-Moslem is forbidden unless he converts, but…"

I interrupted her. "A Moslem *man* may marry a non-Moslem woman…"

"Dear, this is another false rule brought into Islam," Baba asserted. "In reality, one of Mohammad's daughters married a non-Moslem. Still, he welcomed them to his home. Our Prophet never encouraged, or forced them to accept his faith, Islam."

"Then, would you approve of my marriage to a non-Moslem?" I proffered.

"Of course, as long as you love the person," Baba nodded. "There is one God. And all the religious roads lead to Him. It doesn't matter which road we take. Every prophet in different times came to *unite* us to follow his path of love and peace."

Baba paused. "When we unite, then we're stronger as a nation."

"Baba, is this the reason you called your newspaper, *Defa-e-moshtarek?*

"Yes. *United, We Stand,*" his delightful smile soon vanished under the cloud of sorrow when he continued, "a dictatorship regime, like ours, only interested in disuniting the people."

I looked into his sharp eyes. "And it doesn't matter who takes over the country."

He nodded, "Exactly!"

"Nima," Maman jumped in, "stop diverting from the subject." She turned to me. "Then what happened?"

"As I was saying," Baba turned a deaf ear to her, glanced at me and said, "every prophet's purpose is to unite us in the road of spirituality."

"Father," I reminded him, "this isn't the case in today's world."

He nodded. "This is the reason we are called the 'Lost Generation' because of our extreme attraction to the materialistic world." He smiled triumphantly.

"But, dear Mitra," Maman uttered, "you never told us what happened. Ali was studying at Georgetown University, wasn't he?"

"Yes. The problem was," I winced, "I was finishing my degree within six months, but he had at least four more years to go. He was in DC, and I was in LA. He wanted me to marry him under one condition."

Baba frowned. "A condition for marriage is never a good sign, anyway,"

Maman Iran moved closer to me to hear better. "What was that?"

"A crazy proposal" I replied. "After finishing my degree, I would return to Iran, and wait for his arrival until he'd come and marry me."

Maman had a hard time believing her ears. "Four years... wasn't he aware that in marriage, it must be *now* or never?"

The three of us burst out laughing.

―⌐ ⌘ ⌐―

Here in Zurich, I admired my father. Like Ormazd, he also gave me the autonomy to choose my future husband. During ancient Persia, girls had a right to choose their husbands, and decide what to do for their professions. They could even serve in the military. I was joyful that my father still adheres to those ancient rules.

The events of my past occupied my mind. To cheer myself up, I thought about my future. Tomorrow, this time, I would have the seal of the new American Visa in my passport, and soon I'd be flying over there. Being alone in a foreign land made it difficult to not contemplate the reason I escaped my beloved home country. Or perhaps it was the force of Fate.

One early evening a few months ago, when I was a professor at the University of Tehran, I had finished grading the last paper and was getting ready to leave. My office door banged open, startling me. I raised my head. One of my students, Mohsen, rushed in. His face with a thick beard and mustache, an Islamic look for men in contrast to their shaven faces during the Shah's regime, alarmed me. In addition, his red-furious eyes were horrifying. He placed his hands on my desk and leaned forward. His cigarette breath was repulsive.

"Professor," he snarled, "you've become Westernized! After studying in America, you've forgotten how to be a Moslem woman."

To counter his aggression, I calmed myself by wiping my face that was getting wet from his spit of yelling. Then, I said in a friendly voice, "Have a seat, Mohsen. What do you mean?"

He ignored my words and hollered, "We got rid of the corrupt Shah and welcomed the Light of Allah, Khomeini, to have an Islamic regime. Now, *you* must cover your head, and remove your nail polish too. I'll bet you don't pray either, Mrs. Tehrani, do you?"

I did not to let him take me off guard. I said in a confident voice, "Who told you I was educated in America?"

"Your speech, or manner of dressing shows you were in America," he spat.

He was right. My English accent did not sound like the Iranian professors who studied in England. Also, I had on a dark blue suit and skirt out of denim with a cotton light blue blouse underneath, no baggy gray or black outfit like most of the other professors.

I remained quiet. Mohsen took my silence as an insult and banged his fists on the desk while screaming, "America brainwashes our women! Trains them to act like theirs. To be carefree, and not to mind their men!"

"Do you mean to have a mind of their own?" I countered.

"Why aren't you wearing a *hijab?*" He blasted at me as if he was ordering his maid.

In a sturdy voice, I exclaimed, "Who says I have to cover my head?"

"Aren't you a Moslem?" he challenged.

"Yes…"

He didn't let me finish and rushed shouting. "Prophet Mohammad, God Bless his soul, instructs women to cover up!"

Even though this look-alike gorilla intimidated me, the only way out was to engage him even deeper into our dialogue. "Where did you read our Prophet's instruction?"

Mohsen in a quick move dried his sweat that was about to drip on my desk from his forehead. "In the Koran!"

"Are you sure?"

"Yes," he rumbled. "if you take the time and read our holy book, you'd see."

"If you bring me the Koran and show me where Mohammad commanded women to wear hijab, I'll give you an 'A' in the course."

He stood up straight and put his right hand in his pocket.

As if my heart would jump out at any moment, I feared the worst. He suspected he had an impossible task. I worried that he might attack me with a knife, or even a handgun. In those days, the gossip in the street was that most men carried some kind of deadly weapon.

During the Shah's regime, only civilian men were allowed to buy hunting rifles after they would clear the stiff government background check. However, there was no permit issued for a handgun to anyone, except to the military personnel. *But not now.*

My heart thumping increased when Mohsen pulled out a switchblade. His thumb caressed the release button and gave me a feeling that my end was near. I somehow mustered all my strengths and found the courage to stare into his eyes without flinching. In an instant, unclear to me and to my disguised relief, he put the knife back into his pocket.

Within, I was shaking like a willow tree caught in a storm. Outward, I kept my cool appearance, and continued, "Mohsen, the pillar of Islam is based on equality. As our prophet proclaims, 'God creates men and women all, and they are equal to His eye.'"

That caught him off guard and he said. "Professor, where did you read that?"

"After you study Islam! Then you too understand the Islam. Our leaders and politicians have made our Prophet's instructions murky for their own benefits."

He stopped coming back at me. With his head down, he turned and left my office.

That same evening, on my way home, I was proud to douse a man's fury. More than an hour late, I got off the bus. My parents were standing at the bus stop with anxious faces. To see Maman was covered from head to toe in her black *chador* shocked me.

I must get used to seeing her in our traditional cover. I'll never follow this new rule, regardless of who orders me.

They rushed over and hugged me. On the way home, I explained the cause of my delay. Maman raised her head and hands to the sky. "Dear Mitra, thank Allah!" Her voice was clearly quivering. "He didn't attack you with or without his knife."

The numbness in my body became clear to me. "Yes, his better judgment prevented him. Or maybe he decided not to harm a woman, a weak creature."

"Dear Mitra," Baba whispered, "how about going back to America? I'm afraid you won't be safe here."

Wow! To keep me safe, Baba agrees to send me to an unknown land, rather than remaining home.

The night before my big day in Zurich, I went to bed early with high hopes. Soon I would fly to my final destination, the United States of America, the beacon of freedom in the world.

2

THE NEXT MORNING, during my journey to the American Consulate, I was mindful of my every step. I had to be dreaming. The familiar world of yesterday was changing and running away from me. The colorful flowers in front of the *Hauptbahnhof*, the main train station, were hiding from the rain by bowing their heads down in the storm, like the veiled women in my birth country. Over there, most of the women, regardless of their age, obey their male guardians until they marry, and then their husbands are in charge of them.

I stopped when I noticed the American emblem, an eagle holding olive branches, a symbol of peace. The sign on the wall was an affirmation that I'd arrived. After climbing all the thirteen stairs to the second floor, leaving my umbrella behind the door, I touched my brown, shoulder-length hair to make sure every wisp was in place. *Not to have a head like Medusa*, I thought. The past is dead and tomorrow hasn't yet arrived. *I must concentrate on NOW.* The small chrome-handle door diminished my churning inside.

"Good morning!" The cheerful face of the blond-haired, blue-eyed receptionist, shined like the sun on this gloomy day, and made me smile readily. After filling out a pile of paperwork, the same lady guided me to an unoccupied office. She pointed to the two chairs before a mahogany desk. "Please have a seat." And she left.

I had a slight chill. The thick fog blanketed the two

windows at the far right. The room was unwelcoming. A photo of President Carter on the wall was the only remedy for the dismal space. The American flag in the corner warmed up my heart. I had to wiggle in the uncomfortable chair as if thistles covered it. My life-long goal of being a professor in Iran abruptly ended with no fault of my own, and it had been turned upside down.

The events of the previous year rattled in my head. The Shah of Iran, Mohammad Reza Pahlavi, a modernist king, was ousted, after ruling for close to four decades. His expelling put an end to the 2,500-year-old Persian Empire. The Shah used to trumpet in our ears the majestic past times of Cyrus the Great, and Darius the Great. He constantly boasted that he wished to revive the Iranian past glory. At this time, however, his trumpet was silenced. My heartache became unbearable.

Trickles of rain tapping on the pane transported me back to my solitude at the American Consulate. To bring my mind at ease while waiting, I moved my palms together and held them in front of me, closed my deep brown eyes, and recited my mantra. *By connecting with my brain, heart, and hand, I create a unity adequate to heal, awaken, and liberate all I am now.* This way, I brought together the power of logic, emotion, and moving parts to form a triangle within me to conceive that no one or anything can knock me down. I believed. *I am the Master of my destiny.*

The abrupt sound of the door being flung open, followed by several heavy footsteps gave me a jolt. I opened my eyes, stood up, and straightened my knee-high skirt.

"Mitra Tehrani?" Without waiting for any confirmation, he proceeded, "I am James Herald, the Consul." His blank stare made me shiver. And his shiny crewcut hair grabbed my scrutiny. His black suit and crisp white shirt with a dull blue tie marked him as an uncompromising man.

Out of politeness, I offered my hand for a greeting, but he made no effort to return my gesture. It appalled me and I bit my lower lip. The taste of blood kept me present.

He was still standing when he opened the file he carried in his right hand and fixated on its contents as if I were invisible. At last, he lifted his head. His eyebrows knotted with fury in his eyes. He yelled. "Until my fifty-two associates and colleagues are released by your people, I WILL NOT! I WILL NOT let you go to MY country." He wagged his index finger at me like a mean teacher punishing his student.

I've always known that I'm responsible only for my own actions. Now, I'm seen to be representing my entire country. I felt my chest tightening and the ground looked like it was shifting beneath my feet. I lingered with my inside voice. *Besides, I despise what those Persian students did. Why have I become responsible for their crucial act?* I felt nauseated and choked back my opinions when his angry voice startled me again.

"No way, I will renew your visa." His nostrils vibrated like a spent horse after running a race.

Why not, sir? No words, however, left my lips. The slamming door on his way out shook me to my core.

Only three months ago, I could've gotten to America, before President Carter with a stroke of a pen had nullified Iranians' visas. It wasn't meant for me to leave Iran at that time. I was waiting to receive my exit visa from the Iranian government.

A few minutes later, I found myself outside while trying to prevent the teardrops on my cheeks. My father's words came back to me. "Do not cry in any problematic situation. There is always a remedy for everything in this world, except for death."

The rain had stopped. After I took a deep gasp, I wandered the sidewalks. A heavy load in my chest made my breathing more severe. My allergy-induced wheezing tore at my body. I invariably had this irritating cough but never learned why. Back home, Maman Iran, like most other Persians, dismissed it, saying over and over, "Mitra, it's just a cold."

I advanced to linger south of Dufourstrasse, then curved west, chasing the smell of water like a hound dog. A short distance ahead, Zurich-Horn Park was wooing me. Not over five people were in the park. The sight of a few swans gliding on the lake was enticing. To seek solitude and have a break from the hacking cough, I chose a bench next to last in the long line of empty benches. A short time later, out of the corner of my eye, I saw a Middle Eastern man pass me and sit on the furthest pew. I dismissed my nagging, odd feeling. Since I left the Consulate, I thought someone was following me.

I drowned my thoughts in ancient Persia. I could easily identify with the Persian group that left Persia to escape the execution of Zoroastrians during the Arabs' invasion and conquest of my homeland in the seventh century. They were under the leadership of Reverend Mitra, who had the same name as mine. If my forefathers were part of her group, *now* I'd live in India, and at least be with my family and friends, instead of roaming in a foreign country. I called on the brave Reverend to aid me in my unknown path. She appeared to me in her white cloak and shiny eyes. With her strength and wisdom, she led the group of Persians who did not want to leave their ancestors' religion, out of the Arabs' coercion and situated them in Jamnagar, India. Even so, to this day, they have been living in peace and harmony, just like milk and honey. As a woman, I identified with Reverend Mitra. Her victory made me proud. She used her wisdom instead of a sword. A beam of hope ignited in me.

However, the dreary weather in the park and my disappointment at the American Consulate were heavy loads of sorrow on my shoulders. Unlike the Reverend, who had her 200 followers, I was a woman alone without a country, home, family, or friends. At least in this moment of despair, if I were in Tehran, I could smell the delicious scent of blooming lilacs.

I realized the uncertainty in my life was the worst punishment. My future like a dark tunnel stretched before me. Then again, I knew well I was gambling with my future when I left my home country.

Maman's teary eyes flashed before me, taking me back to several months ago in Tehran.

"Dear Mitra, you've fulfilled all the wishes your father and I had for you. You've earned the highest degree and are now a professor." She let out a sigh. "One more wish, I would very much like to see my grandchildren before leaving this world."

Then, my father added, "Your Mom is asking you to sign the contract with the university and stay here."

I got a wave of exasperation and announced, "How do you expect me to put my name on such a bizarre contract, obligating me to concede to this ridiculous rule of wearing a hijab?"

"Mitra," Maman's speech came louder, "they're not killing you, are they?"

Sometimes to be killed can be a blessing. I thought.

My words like bullets left my mouth. "YOU didn't have to cover your head, did you? Nor your mother. You had a choice." I countered. "Why do I need to abide by a rule that takes me back to the seventh century?"

"By ordering women to cover their heads," Baba spoke in my defense, "this fanatical regime robs women of their individual freedom."

"They've tongue-tied us." I asserted. "Father, Iranian women had the same freedom as men in ancient times. Women did not cover their heads in Persia. They were on an even keel with men. Also, Mohammad never instructed women to cover their heads. Then why must women wear hijab *now?*"

"You're right, Mitra," Baba agreed. "As far as we know, none of Mohammad's daughters covered their heads either."

"As history has it," Maman proclaimed, "they even took part in battles against their tribe."

I repeated my question, "Why now? Are we going backward, instead of forward?"

"The clergymen and politicians brought the hijab, a Turkish custom, was forced to the Moslem women," Baba replied.

Maman only shook her head and in the protest said, "Mitra! For once why don't you just do what you're told?"

"You know me well, I can't help but be defiant."

She looked into space and with a sad voice uttered, "Perhaps, if our lives stayed as simple as it was in the past, then it wouldn't be such a big deal for you to cover your head and abide by the law of land."

I confirmed with a head movement. "If the Shah and his father didn't modernize our land, the women would be still staying home, taking care of their children, and reading only the Koran in Arabic. *And* they continued to be submissive to their men."

Baba in a smirky smile, said, "And men were much happier to have female slaves."

"I know your father is kidding," Maman mumbled. "It seems like in the modern times, women are getting the short end of the stick. I have my work inside the house and my job outside."

"Aren't you happy, Maman?" But before she could answer, I went on, "You have economical freedom. Now as a retired teacher, whenever you are not pleased with Baba, you can divorce him and live your life."

"Thanks to Islam," Baba injected. "Mohammad gave men and women the right of divorce equally."

"But we all know," Maman's anger was obvious. "In this culture, we compare a divorcee to a rotten watermelon." When she saw my bewildered eyes, she said. "You know, like a prostitute, and it's always the woman's fault, in case of a divorce."

"And it's sad that most women do not have any idea that our Prophet has given voice to them. Besides, why do we have to listen to some ignorant people?" I countered.

"Wow!" Maman responded. "You've become very Westernized, my dear."

"In a democratic society, women must have the same rights as men. Isn't that what the new regime promised us?" I paused when my attention went to Baba's moving hands, signaling us to bring our voices down.

Maman ignored Baba and roared, "We women willingly embrace our Ayatollah Khomeini's command to cover our heads."

"If it's a choice, then why are they giving me a contract to sign," I demanded, "instead of leaving it up to me?"

"Have you talked with some of your colleagues," Baba whispered, "to learn whether they will sign it or not?"

"There are not very many women among us. However, most of them signaled they'll do," I said through my clenched teeth.

"Well, they're smart," Maman said vehemently, "To feed their family is more important than revolting against a force they never…"

"Fraulein, Miss!"

Broken from my reverie, I raised my head and noticed the Middle Eastern man was standing before me.

From his appearance, he did not look like a lowlife. The scar on his left cheek seemed familiar, but I refused to pressure my memory and figure out who he was.

"Are you Persian?"

I confirmed only with a nod. The bucket of my strength for any conversations was empty. Likely, he was nosy and wanted to learn why I was in Switzerland, or when I got here.

"Salam, Hello!" He was persistent.

I turned my face, got up without a word, and took a few steps closer to the swans. The mother swan was trying to teach the seven little ones how to swim. It did not seem the cold water bothered them. Their tiny peddling feet showed their desire for life. The mother swan was absorbed on her duty. These exquisite creatures could not possibly survive in Iran. It is too hot and too suffocating for them. All at once, the uncertainty of my life hit me like a hammer.

To go home... or not to go!

3

IN MY HOTEL room, I paced the floor all night long, wondering how I could stay in Switzerland. In despair, while picking my pajamas out of the suitcase, I touched a soft silky fabric. Its warm vibrations flow through my body. *Ah-ha!* It's *soozany*, the shawl. My mother had to leave it there while I was getting dressed. The smell of rosewater filled the room, a reminder of Aziz's scent. As if it was yesterday.

As a little girl, I bonded with my great-grandmother, Aziz. My grandmother, Shirin, had died way before my birth. Every month, Maman Iran took me on a three-hour bus ride to Shahriar, a village south of Tehran to visit Aziz.

The memory of traveling in those old buses made me smile. Maman always paid extra for the tickets to sit behind the driver, to be safe. I had a perfect view of the passengers getting on and off. Their coarse outfits were a clear sign of them being peasants. Almost every man and woman wore black cotton baggy pants with loose tops. Many of the women had a floral fluffy tutu with fake coins hanging from it. With their every move, they jingled. With no exception, every woman wore a headscarf or chador, except Maman. She always dressed as if she stepped out of a Parisian fashion magazine. Her tailored checkered skirt and long sleeve blouse looked elegant. And she pinned her coiffured curly hair away from her face. No one knew that every six months, her skillful beautician made her straight hair curly. To mount the bus took a long time for the women, as everyone

21

had to shove her own hefty bundle through the door and down the aisle. The driver's assistant turned a blind eye to helping any of them, not even to take their hands or to lift them from under their arms.

"Maman!" I inquired, "Why doesn't he help these women up into the bus?"

"Dear," Maman's expression clouded, "he's forbidden to touch them."

"Why not?"

"In Islam, a man who isn't a brother, uncle, or husband may not touch a woman."

"Even to assist her!"

Maman nodded.

The men climbed in easily, for they had no heavy loads. They were only carrying their chickens and roosters under their arms or in long cages. Once in a while, a farmer had a small goat or sheep with no leash. The animal never left its owner's side as if it was his pet. I imagined we were only missing a couple of tigers and lions. Then, our bus would certainly have made a very fun circus.

When I was ten years old, upon our arrival, Aziz summoned me to sit on the edge of her bed. She pulled the shawl from under her pillow with a shaky and fragile hand, gave it to me, and in a weak voice said, "My dear," she breathed, "this soozany is my gift to you."

It was a blessing to have the shawl with me in Zurich tonight. Aziz's voice sounded in my ears again, "This soozany has traveled through time, from many generations ago. We sat on it to get married, and cried into it when we lost a loved one."

Aziz sighed, and with a shade of smile she continued, "or held on to it while giving birth."

Here tonight almost eighteen years later, I had not done what Aziz, or other women did while they owned the shawl, no marriage or giving birth to my credit. I covered my shoulders with it and felt as if I'd reached an oasis. The soozany served me as a sanctuary. Its vibrant silk threads interwoven with silver and gold strings generated an alluring feeling in me, especially with its paisley patterns. This piece of heaven connected me with all the women who came before me. I had to admit. It warmed my body and soul. *I feel alone no more.*

In an instant, I had a sense of clarity and hope, no longer frightened by being between the two extremes of the East and the West, or by the tragedy of our monarchy termination. I repeated my mantra to help me concentrate and create *unity within*. My breathing became easier as if the shawl had uplifted my spirit. To think of the female groundbreakers cheered me up, and made me forget my own upheaval. At once I envisioned Reverend Mitra encouraging me to stay away from subjugation and choose the path of freedom regardless of how difficult it would be.

The next day, when I opened my eyes in Zurich, I didn't believe how well I had slept. I arose humming. The sun was radiant and beckoned me to a new day. A pair of beige slacks and a soft pink blouse with short sleeves concealed my anxiety. I spent no time on drying or straightening my hair. I left its natural curls be.

As I stepped outside, the aroma of coffee from a nearby cafe beckoned me. It was surprising to see a bookstore next door. *Wow! Never noticed it before.* Without hesitation, I hurried through its revolving door. Suddenly, my right ankle twisted causing me to slip, very close to hitting the marble floor. If it wasn't for a powerful hand grabbing my arm, I would for sure have fallen and broken some bones. I raised my head to thank the man, but he was no where to be found. I had only a glance of his brown jacket.

Inside the store, I immersed myself in the ocean of books. *They feed my soul.* Like an anxious merchant in the Bazar looking for a precious gem among hundreds and hundreds of rags, I started eyeing the books. The picturesque book, *Unser 20 Jahhundert, Our 20th Century*, captured my curiosity. I picked it up from the display and flipped through it. An old picture taken in 1952 showed the young Shah and his second, gorgeous wife, Soraya. Her father was a Kurdish chief, and her mother was German. A set of perfect ebony eyebrow arches framed her eyes. The Queen's dark, wavy short hair in perfect shape enhanced her milky face. Her beauty, a mixture of the East and the West, was astonishing.

It was obvious that the Shah married her because of her Kurdish background. This tribe has been one of the strongest tribes in Iran. Most of the time, the tribes uprose against the central government. A king only saved his crown when he held them down by force or shook hands with them. However, the commoners heard she was the love of his life.

Soraya's misfortune came when she was unable to instill the crown for the Shah with a son. After their divorce, she left Iran. The talk on the street was that she had asked the Shah to abdicate like King Edward VIII, the British monarch, who had voluntarily left the crown for his brother, to spend the rest of his life with his American lover. The Shah, however, preferred to hold on to his throne rather than leaving with Soraya.

I looked at the picture again. They were sitting in a less-fortunate farmer's room observing the space, a photo op, no doubt. There was no sign of the peasant or his family.

Perhaps if the Shah was more sympathetic to the working class, he wouldn't have such a downcast destiny. A few years later, in order to uproot the feudalism in Iran, the Shah deeded out his own properties to the laborers who farmed in his land.

In a documentary film, a farmer, first in a line of famers, approaches the Shah and receives the deed. After the Shah shakes his hand, the farmer kneels down to His Majesty and kisses his feet.

At the end of the picture, my father grumbled. "Of course, they're not showing that the Shah has already received the money from the treasury and had sent it to his accounts in Swiss banks."

"In addition," Maman followed Baba's words. "no one asks him, when and how *he* became the owner of so many land parcels."

Baba delighted that Maman was in agreement with him. With a smirk, he said, "His father was only a simple soldier and no one had any idea that he or his family was such a wealthy landlord."

As a teenager, confusion took over me. I had no idea who to believe, the media portraying the Shah as a benevolent king, or Baba's belief that His Majesty was only after his own personal and monetary gains. Baba said over and over. "This traitor is milking the Iranian people."

In the Zurich library, I remembered that many nerve-racking events have transpired since that photograph. A year after that picture, the Shah and Soraya left the country because our only elected prime minister, Mossadegh, had sought to cut the Western arms and create an independent democratic country. He was also decisive in cutting back the Shah's power.

One afternoon during our usual stroll in downtown, my father and I came across throngs of demonstrators, all men in distressed outfits, looking angry. They were carrying several placards showing the Shah and Queen Soraya, along with our green, white, and red flag, illustrating a gold lion holding a sword, protecting the crown rising from its back. They were shouting, "Long live our King, and Queen!" Other words which I could not comprehend accompanied their uproars. I had to cover my ears. Then, immediately, Baba scooped me from the ground and put me down on the other sidewalk, away from the protestors.

"Let's wait here until they're gone."

I looked at his worried face and asked, "Baba, are these mobs going to attack us?"

"No, no!"

"Why are they screaming?"

He caressed my head. "They're crying out for the Shah's return, and demanding Mossadegh's resignation."

A few days later, with the aide of a group led by the head of the military, and with the support of the CIA, the Shah returned to his people. Unfortunately, the only elected Prime Minister, Mossadegh, who had the people's interest in heart, was arrested like a criminal and sentenced to house arrest until his death.

The Shah of Iran, *Shahan Shah*, King of Kings, the successor of King Cyrus the Great, who gave his life fighting to free slaves, was now spending his days in self-exile with his third wife, Empress Farah. She was fruitful and gave birth to our Crown Prince.

The Persian royals have spent the last year wandering the world trying to find a home. First, they set out to America due to the Shah's declining health, an underlying reason for him to leave Iran. Almost every year, the palace announced: "His Majesty is taking a trip to Europe for his check-up." *As if an Iranian Medical facility is only sufficient for the commoners, but it's beneath His Majesty.*

But this time, the Shah's trip to America made Khomeini furious. To test the strength of ties between the Shah and the American president, he demanded to extradite the Shah. In spite of accepting Khomeini's sovereignty regime, President Carter refused to do so. Then, with or without Khomeini's support, some students attacked the American embassy in Tehran. As the result, the Shah was forced to leave one of his long-term allies' land. Ever since, the King without a country has been traveling through countries where he sought a safe haven.

To everyone's surprise, Anwar Sadat, the Egyptian president, granted the Shah asylum, and was not afraid of Khomeini's wrath. *Unbelievable!* The two countries' animosity went back to the time when the Shah was a crown prince. His father, Reza Shah, a soldier, came to power by coup d'e'tat and removed the previous dynasty, my maternal grandfather, Ali Khan's linage. Reza Shah persuaded his son to marry the Egyptian princess, the king's sister, Fawzia, to strengthen the relationship between the two countries.

According to some rumors, the royal marriage was far from being a happy one. The obvious reason was that the Egyptian Princess gave birth to a girl who was not a guarantee for the continuation of the Pahlavi Dynasty. Of course, a girl seldom became a ruler. We had only three queens as heads of state all through the Persian Empire before the Arabs conquered Persia. Even though the Shah had a twin sister, a few minutes older than he was, she was pushed aside, and he became the King.

While Reza Shah was alive, no one could breathe a word. His end of life was not that much better than his son's. During the last years of Reza Shah's governing, Hitler was devouring one country after another. At one point, he held his eyes on Russia and crossed over to its borders. The Allies' strategy, specifically Churchill's, was to bring their forces through Iran from the Persian Gulf in the South, then to the North to battle Hitler's forces in Russia. They requested our King's permission. He was a famous ruler known for his 'Iron-fist' and knew Persians were the same race as Germans, Aryans, so he refused to unite with the Western leaders in opposition to Hitler.

Soon, the Allies believed Reza Shah was a Hitler sympathizer. Then, the people heard: our King abdicated in favor of his son and retired to Morris Island.

A tapestry, no matter how thick it is, cannot cover the truth for very long. Within a brief time, Reza Shah, after standing up against the Western forces, had to pay a severe price. He was compelled to hand over his crown to his oldest son, the Shah of Iran. His 'Iron-fist' worked only for Iranians, not for the Western leaders.

In 1943, the Allies leaders: Franklin Roosevelt, Winston Churchill, and Joseph Stalin met in Tehran and worked out a strategy to defeat Hitler by putting boots on the ground throughout our beloved homeland from the South to the North. They confronted no resistance from our young King. In return, the benevolent Allies leaders recognized Iran's independency. Since then, the Shah became one of the Western supporters, known in Iran, as a *puppet of the West*. Everyone seemed to forget that the Allies were the ones who seated His Majesty on his throne.

In 1944, after Reza Shah died in exile, his body was sent

via Egypt to Iran. Before the Egyptian king permitted the release of Reza Shah's coffin, he demanded Fawzia's divorce decree. The dialogue was belligerent and intense. At last, the two sides settled. Until a few years ago, these two countries had been antagonists. The commoners never know what goes on behind the curtain of politics. Notably, in countries like mine.

In the Swiss bookstore, dark clouds covered my heart. I ignored Iranians despairing past and looked for books in English. I stumbled upon a small one, a translation of my favorite German poet, Rainer Maria Rilke. After opening it, the first quotation riveted me:

> *Perhaps all dragons of our lives are only princesses,*
> *Who are waiting to see us once, beautiful and brave!*

I repeated under my breath, *I must be brave.* My gut feelings warned me not to go back to the country where the regime treats its people like cattle, especially the women, shoved and prodded to the pleasure of its leaders. I promised myself to never return to my beloved country while the fanatical regime was in power. *I must also put a lid on my desires to see my family, friends, and even my beloved books.*

It was only a few months ago. I was still in Iran. My parents and I attended the funeral of one of Maman's friends at Beheshteh Zahra, the largest cemetery in Tehran, the size of several football stadiums. After the cab driver let us out at the main gate, we started hiking for at least twenty minutes. As we were passing grave after grave, I noticed each headstone was decorated with the 10"x10" framed picture of the deceased, all young men. I did not trust my eyes, so I bent over to read the dates of their birth and death. Not one of them was over twenty-five years old.

I inquired, "Baba, how come all these young ones are dead?"

In a low voice, he responded, "Since this government has taken power, they've massacred more youths in opposition to the regime than the Shah killed during his entire reign." He sighed with no sound.

I was surprised. "You don't care for this government either, do you?"

"I'm quite disappointed," Baba answered. "We hoped that one day, we'd have a government to guide us toward democracy, not to force us to go backward."

"Like our proverb," I said. "We came to fix her eyebrows, instead we blinded her."

"Instead of creating an egalitarian society, we brought theocracy to replace dictatorship," Baba whispered and kept quiet the rest of the way.

While riding in the cab on our way back, I suggested stopping by my grandfather, Ali Khan's mausoleum, and pay our respects. Baba, sitting by the driver, turned and stared at me. Suddenly, Maman's tears rolled down on her face.

"You don't know what happened," Baba murmured.

His response confused me. "No! What?"

"I'll tell you when we get home," he replied.

When we arrived home at sunset, Maman went to the back yard wash up for prayers, I took this opportunity to ask, "Baba, why didn't we stop at Grandpa's grave and send some *salavat* to his soul?"

Sadly, he replied, "This hierocracy regime bulldozed all the graves in that cemetery."

"No!" I hit my cheek. "Even my brother, Jahan's?"

Baba bit his knuckles and whispered, "They even sent a paltry sum of money to the surviving family members, sprinkling salt on a wound." He struggled with breathing as if he was carrying a heavy load in his chest.

"And they boast, 'they're sent by God,'" I said bitterly. "So they're trying to make their desecration of graves look legal by paying money."

"Right."

"Is it true, Baba, they even disinterred the former king, Reza Shah's body, burned it, and razed his monument?"

"No," Baba shook his head. "We heard when the Shah fled the country, he reportedly took his father's body with him." Baba lowered his voice. "Dear Mitra, at this time who knows and who cares?"

I bet the Shah's children care.

After that, for several nights I could not even close my eyes for long. Most of the time, my grandfather's and Jahan's bones and skulls being crushed was playing like a horror movie in my mind. *The regime even feared of the dead to raise against them.*

The sharp pain of these memories snapped me back to the present in the bookstore. I was having a difficult time breathing and craved fresh air and open space. I rushed outside.

ON MY WAY out of the bookstore, I heard, "Salam." Before I could react, the fellow added, "Lady Mitra, would you like to have a cup of coffee with me?" The same Persian man with the scar on his left cheek, standing before me asked. His brown jacket caught my attention. He echoed his question like an old gramophone, "Lady Mitra, would you like to have a cup of coffee with me?"

"Sir," my brow furrowed, "do I know you? How do you know my name?"

"I'm Majid Enayati. Do you not recognize me? I have a piece of news from our mutual friend."

"I think You're mistaken," I remembered him but refused to admit it.

"Ben Amirian, does it sound familiar?"

To learn his name caused me to think as if the earth had stopped turning. I could no longer deny it. With a dire face, I pressed, "What about him?"

"Please, let's go inside." He stepped toward the nearby coffee house without waiting for a response from me.

The buzzing cafe sounded like a beehive. "Get us a table." Majid's calm voice drove me to trust him. "I'll get us some tea."

While combing through the crowd for an unoccupied table, and two chairs, Ben's handsome face flashed before my eyes, and I wondered what he was doing. When a table at a secluded corner became vacant, I sat down and let my mind fly to him.

I had met him and Majid in Rome last December. PanAm Airline, partly retained by the Shah, had ended its direct flights from New York to Tehran because of the hostage situation. I had to stop somewhere in Europe. In reply to the agent, I responded, "Rome, Italy. I've never been there and would love to see it."

~ ❦ ~

After my arrival in Rome, the coming day I walked to the Vatican to visit the Sistine Chapel. Like a docile pupil, I carried out what my professor had suggested. "Lie down on the floor and become *one* with Michelangelo's 'Creation of Adam,' and all the other majestic paintings around you. Let your eyes have a feast."

I imagined being in paradise, oblivious to the individuals around me coming and going. I overheard a male voice in Farsi: "See, Majid, look! Only a Western girl stretches out in public on the floor like this." Then the two men broke out chuckling.

When I bolted upright, I saw a dashing young man who looked very much like Omar Sharif without his mustache, standing and beaming at me with his undaunted shiny eyes. My reaction to him was so intense that it led my breathing to flutter rapidly.

"Oops! Lady, you are Iranian! I'm Behnam Amirian. Call me Ben, and this is Majid Enayati. Sorry for disturbing you," he declared as a smile lighted his clean-shaven visage. His stylish fitted trench coat enveloped his tall fit structure, leaving no defiance in me. In an instant, I forgot all my shyness and wet my lips.

"You had to be new. I haven't seen an elegant lady like you around here," Ben stated, while his eyes pierced my heart.

34

I nodded.

"How long have you been in Rome?"

"I arrived last night." My face became flushed and hot. Thanks to my olive skin, no one could identify how apprehensive I was.

Ben looked at his watch and spoke in a polite and earnest expression. "It's lunchtime. Are you hungry?" His confident words tied my tongue, no objection from me.

Ben, encouraged, continued, "An Italian restaurant with delicious food is close by, as a newcomer in Rome, you should try it."

"Okay." I blinked my eyes in disbelief at my response. I'd just accepted the invitation of a complete stranger. *In a foreign land, no one is a stranger as long as they're from my country.* I convinced myself.

"Let's go." Ben showed the way.

The three of us walked to Ben's car. As a gentleman, Majid insisted that I sit in the front and he took the back seat.

The restaurant was a fancy one with its white tablecloths. The host guided us to a booth. Soon a server put an Antipasti platter in the middle of the table. Then, another one brought us a basket of cut bread and poured olive oil in our side dishes. During our conversations, in Italian, Ben ordered a bottle of wine. After being in the West for several years, I still had a habit of not drinking wine or beer during the day. To my mind, only alcoholics do that. So, Ben, ordered me sparkling water.

To my surprise, Ben also educated in America, and was a senior diplomat to the Iranian embassy here. And Majid was his assistant.

With a laugh, Ben said, "It's funny, I don't know your name yet."

"Mitra Tehrani."

"Mitra, how long are you staying here?"

"Two days."

"Why such a short time?"

"I must be in Tehran to start my teaching job."

"Are you a professor?" Majid shot me a surprised look.

I nodded without taking my eyes off Ben.

While eating, Ben and I conversed. As if we were the only ones at the table. Before dessert, Majid excused himself and left. The scar on his cheek was the only sign etched in my memory.

By this time, I felt at ease with Ben as if I'd known him for my entire life. It was unusual for me to like a man in a heartbeat. I felt butterflies in my stomach at his suggestion to be my tour guide and show me the Eternal City. I took him as my friend and trusted him. Besides, here everyone was a stranger and could not pass a judgment on me. I could hear the gossips if Ben and I were in Iran.

Oh, gosh! I saw Mitra in a restaurant sitting next to a young man. His mouth was at her ear, and their hands were under the table. Allah knows what they were doing down there.

I shook myself, turned to Ben with a cheerful face, and responded, "Fantastic," I could do a happy dance right then and there.

All afternoon as Ben drove, he explained and pointed out Rome's many majestic sites, the Forum, Pantheon Temple, the Colosseum, and Trevi Fountain.

"This is a distinguished fountain," Ben expressed and reached for my hand and pulled it to his chest. "Let's park the car and walk around."

Enthralled, I could only move my lips. "Okay."

"If you wish to return to Rome in a year," Ben directed, "throw a coin in the fountain and your wish will come true."

"Really? I don't believe it."

He grinned. "Why don't you do it just for the fun of it?"

"Impossible," I frowned. "I'm on my way to Iran, and I don't have any plan to return soon."

"I'll toss a coin in and wish for your return to me, even sooner than a year." Ben gently pulled me closer and held me tight. Our giggles filled the piazza.

I did not know how long it was until Majid carrying a tray approached me.

"I got some pastries too." He placed the tray between us and sat down.

"Thank you."

As he picked up one of the cups, I asked, "Do you still see Ben?"

In slow-motion, he put a coup down before me and the other for himself. Then, he did the same with the pastries. Like a deaf person, he left to return the tray. My patience was boiling over. When he returned and took his seat, with no control, I blurted out, "To tell you the truth, I'm very much over Ben!"

"How come?"

"He promised to call and come to see me in Tehran within a month or so."

"Did he not call?"

"Yes, he did a few times, but then the phone calls stopped," I said irritably. "No news at all. The first few months I was furious and tried to forget him. Did he fall in love with an Italian girl?"

Majid shook his head and his face turned pale. "I couldn't believe I ran into you yesterday, twice in two days after almost over a year."

"Where is Ben? Is he still in Rome?" My hope of seeing Ben again sparkled in my heart.

Majid took a sip of his tea. "Please have some tea and sweets."

"Tell me." I stopped. It was laborious for me to get the words out. "Do you still see him?"

"I have to tell you something," Majid hesitated, "but I don't know how."

"What is it? Is he married?"

"Ben is," his voice trembled as he looked down, "Ben is dead."

The world collapsed on my head. I felt tears on my cheeks. Through them, I asked, "What happened?"

He said in a somber voice, "a few months after you left, he received a call from our foreign ministry summoning him back to Tehran…"

Oh, he came to Tehran and didn't even call me.

"When he got there, two *mojahedin*, Islamic police, right away picked him up at the airport." Majid paused. "They accused him of espionage, put him in jail, and after a mock trial, they hung him in private. Even his family could not get his body."

My head throbbed. "Was he a spy? Didn't the new regime appoint him?"

Majid shrugged. "Who knows?"

"True, True," I paused. "Over there, the regime does not need a reason for murdering someone."

I felt as if my heart was fragmented. In an instant, all my anger toward Ben evaporated. All this time, I had convinced myself that Ben was a charlatan and wanted only to go to bed with me. My anger morphed into an ocean of sorrow that was drowning me. I rushed to the door and started running like a blinded person.

In my room, I wrapped the soozany, around me and cried into it as my despair crushed my entire body. The difficulty of breathing and nonstop coughing added to my stress. To think of Ben and his death was unbearable.

After I arrived in Tehran from Rome, Ben and I had several lovely phone conversations. No wonder his calls stopped. I tried calling him over and over. All of them went unanswered. The anger spiked in me. My mind dramatized that Ben had no genuine interest in me. At last, I erased him from my memory. *Not an effortless task. I was wronged,* I avowed.

With a bleeding heart, I remembered our first evening in Rome. Ben suggested having dinner at a restaurants surrounding the Trevi Fountain. We reveled in its splendor, the balmy evening breeze whispering through the piazza carried the mist from the fountain and enveloped us in its coolness. After relishing a superb Chianti complementing a delicious Anti-pasta dish and grilled fish, Ben pleaded with me to extend my stay at least another four days. Sitting close to him, I could touch his knee and stare into his obsidian eyes throughout the dinner. *Is it his look, his charm, or simply I'm ready to fall in love?*

For years, I had waited in anticipation to find my *special man*. In America, my studies had always taken priority. I had dated and had a few male friends. I yearned to experience love's joys, to share my body with my lover, and attain the fulfillment of being loved in return.

In Rome, I felt the woman within ready to roar. Ben ignited my inner passion. I had always hoped one day, I could *love*, the way Maman loved Baba Nima, or my grandmother loved Hafiz, the poet of love. *I could love Ben with all my entire being.*

Tonight in Zurich, my hope of seeing Ben, being held by him, curling up with him, or even seeing him again, was all fractured. My resolution hardened, tempered by my anger and anguish. Like a bolt of lightning, I affirmed that I would not return to my homeland as long as this totalitarian regime maintains control of my beloved country. I had confidence in overcoming any obstacles presented to me in this foreign land, *no mountain is too high to climb, and no battle is too fierce to fight.*

∽5∾

AT SUNRISE, I found myself curled in the fetal position with the shawl covering my petite frame. The horror of Ben's death hit me anew. To lift from melancholy, I forced myself to concentrate on Rilke's words once, then:

> *Perhaps the dragons of our lives are princesses,*
> *Who are waiting to see us once, beautiful and brave!*

Suddenly, as if Ben was whispering from heaven, I listened. *My love, act as a hero, and tame your dragons.*

I envisioned Ben in Rome, running down the Spanish stairs. On the last one, he wrapped his muscular arms around my waist, picked me up as if he was moving a feather, held me tight against his broad chest, then gently released me. We walked hand-in-hand toward the Colosseum, remembering the movie, *Spartacus*, the slave who challenged the Legions of Rome and held the country in mortal fear. We whispered to each other, "Never abandon our dreams of being with each other." Just as Spartacus never submitted to Roman tyranny.

After I extended my time in Rome, we drove about two hours south to Gaeta, a quaint medieval town with clean beaches. We were a picture-perfect young couple, happy with fresh love. In the hotel, only three hundred steps to the beach. Where Ben registered us as "Mr. and Mrs. Ben Amirian." It pleased me to no end despite not being true.

The sense of guilt or apprehension was absent in me. Instead, I felt liberated. As a grown woman, I was determined. This was unlike most of the girls from the Iranian culture. They must marry based on their guardian's choice. In Rome, I turned my back on the long-standing tradition.

In my hotel room, I remembered Reverend Mitra. *I must act like her—wise, brave and strong.*

All-day long my body was in Zurich, but the puzzle of how to remain in Switzerland until the political upheaval was settled occupied my mind. I understood well that nothing in this world stays the same. *I must continue the path to freedom.* The only freedom for me was to stay in the Western world.

The following morning, before sunrise, I went to Zurich University. I was a professor in Tehran and held a doctorate degree from America. I figured there must be something for me to do. After a walk of about half an hour, I stood in front of the English Department. I glanced at several office doors to find an American name. *An American professor would likely be more sensitive to my situation.*

I read: "Dr. Phillip Johnson," I failed scan the rest to know his office hours. I waited and waited. My only companion was my recurring coughs. Sometimes, I sat on the floor, leaning against the wall, or standing up, but never strayed from the office. The hallway of the old building was quiet. At sunset, I heard some footsteps climbing the stairs and soon a middle-aged, tall man carrying a briefcase was approaching me.

"Dr. Johnson?" I inquired.

"Yes," he assessed that I'd been waiting a long time. "sorry, after finals, we don't keep our office hours. Please come on in.

I just came to pick up," without letting him finish, I blurted out, "I'm Dr. Mitra Tehrani, a Persian."

While we both were still standing, he raised his head and looked shocked. "How did you get out of that country, especially being a woman?"

"It wasn't easy," I swallowed hard.

Dr. Johnson beckoned me to take the chair facing his desk. "What can I do for you?"

"I fled in opposition to the Khomeini's regime and his laws," I began.

"These days women are not treated kindly over there, are they?"

"No," my sadness was clear in my voice.

He took his seat behind the desk, removed his glasses, and wiped his eyes.

I went on, "I'm refusing to go back and abide by the rules of the oppressive government."

"I don't blame you. Oppression will make even wise men mad." He flinched. "What's your status?"

"I have a visitor visa."

"Here, we only allowed to hire Swiss students," he said. "but, if you change your status to a student, you will have permission to work part-time anywhere."

I was flabbergasted. "How is it possible, Professor?"

He came up with a solution, "Register at the university for your post-doctorate."

"Thank God," I exclaimed, "I brought my transcripts in German and English with me."

"Who is your favorite author?" He inquired.

"John Updike."

"Why?"

"Because he weaves mythology in modern events and creates fabulous fiction."

A smile lit up his face. "It's a fascinating concept, isn't it?"
I smiled in return.

"Describe your reasons for wanting to proceed with your education here in a few pages," he advised, "then, as your major professor, I'll write a letter to the university to explain how it's imperative to mix the ancient time stories into the modern time."

Like milk and honey, I theorized. "Thank you so much, Professor."

"See you within a week." He handed me his card. "This is my number. Call me when you're ready."

I thanked Dr. Johnson, placed his card in my bag, and soon I was wandering the Zurich streets as if in a daze, unable to get excited by the beauty of this city or its fancy shops and restaurants on my way to the hotel.

The next day, after submitting my transcripts to the Admission Office, I walked to the Student Affairs Office. I approached the information desk and said to the receptionist, "Where can I find information on room rentals?"

"Over there." The young student pointed to the wall at her right-hand side.

A few index cards covered the board. I jotted down some names and phone numbers based on their prices. The Central Plaza Hotel could not be my home for much longer. My parents paid for it from Tehran, but now I must save the measly money I brought out of the country allowed by the Iranian government.

Most of the numbers either did not answer, or the place was taken. I dialed what looked to be my last hope. "Hello, Francis. Is the extra room in your flat available?"

"No takers yet," Francis replied. "Whoever comes to see it, says, 'too far to the university.'"

"Is it in the suburb?"

"Yes, very quiet, and one streetcar takes you to the university."

"Can I come and see it now?"

"Any time, I'm here. Your name is?"

"Mitra."

"See you soon."

Francis and Ralph were two cartoonists. Their studio was located across the street from their apartment complex in the suburb of Zurich. Francis lived on the first floor and Ralph occupied the second floor with his slender, high-cheekbones companion from Nairobi, and their two children.

Francis opened the door. His English, mixed with a twang of Swiss-German, sounded cute. He pulled his shoulder-length hair away from his face.

He must be a leftover of the hippies' era. With a wide smile, he unlocked the closest door to the entrance. "This is the one for rent."

The spotless mattress, desk, and chair at the far end of the room, with its wall-to-wall windows made it sufficient for me. Francis' room was next to the first one. Its door was ajar.

"My room is a mess." He closed it in a hurry. Next in the row, there was a tiny space covered in the soft yellow wallpaper and a few books on a bookshelf. "This is my girlfriend, Agnes's sofa," he said, pointing to a tiny two-seater.

"Does she sleep here?"

"No, she comes here when she gets angry with me," he laughed.

"Does she live here too?"

"No, no! Sometimes she visits me."

"Tell you the truth," I turned to him. " I like the place. How much is it per month?"

"150 Swiss Fracs."

The flat was spacious, well lighted, and in a quiet neighborhood.

Francis repeated, "You can catch a trolly car to get to the heart of Zurich or the university."

He and I shook hands on the rental, then I confessed, "I can't pay you right this moment. First, I have to cash my cashier's check."

"No worries." He waved his hand. "In Switzerland, we have many banks. Just go down the street, there is one."

"Do you mind if I bring my suitcase here today? I can't afford to stay in the hotel any longer."

Francis flicked his hand again, "Not at all."

"See you within a couple of hours or so."

"If you need anything, just call me."

I walked a mile farther to a branch of HSBC.

"I would like to cash this cashier check," I said, placing it before the teller.

While his head was down counting some bills, he asked, "Do you have an account with us?"

"No."

"If you don't," the teller said casually, "we can't cash it."

"May I open one?"

The teller gave me a five-page application. I filled it out and returned it to him.

"This is your account number." He pointed to the top of the page. "Which bank has issued the check?"

"Meli Bank, Tehran, Iran."

"Nein! Nein!" he bellowed, as if he had forgotten he was speaking English to me, "We don't accept it. Iran, no way!"

"Over there," I argued, "they told me this is like cash."

He shook his head combatively. "Not from that country!"

Then, he pushed the check on the counter toward me.

Talking with this teller in Zurich reminded me of a similar event that occurred one month after the hostage situation while I was a student at UCLA. As usual, on the first day of every month, I went to the bank to get some cash. At the bank in Los Angeles, the teller after staring me down, called the manager over. A heavy-set man informed me, "Miss Tehrani, your balance is zero."

"Zero?" I said in confusion. "How is it possible?"

"I'm very sorry." The manager held up his hands in a show of helplessness. "The American government has frozen all Iranian assets."

"W-Why?" My cough barely let me get the word out.

"Because of the hostage situation, President Carter ordered a freeze of Iranian assets."

"What does it have to do with my pittance?" I countered. "They ought to go after the Shah and his family's assets, not mine."

"The federal government has the power to pull out the money from any account," the manager said in a cold voice.

For a few days, I got by. Thanks to my American friends. They lent me some cash to survive through the tough time. In no time, like a wildfire, an uproar started by the International Federation for Human Rights, and Amnesty International, protesting for the release of the Iranian students' funds. As a result, all students' money including mine were released. However, the American government kept all the other Iranian assets frozen, up to one-hundred billion dollars in total to punish Khomeini. But, the American government did not realize that in reality, they were punishing the Iranian people.

―⊙⊷⊷⊷⊙―

I had to address my predicament at this moment in Zurich. I murmured, "Sir, what is my remedy?" The Swiss teller's unfriendly eyes made me take a deep breath, and I concentrated on yet another block in my way. I addressed him again in a calm voice, "Sir, I arrived here a few days ago, and right now, this check is all I have."

The teller wanted to help and suggested, "If a Swiss account holder with us, guarantees to cover this check, then we can deposit it in your new account. Also, keep in mind there's a hold on it for at least two weeks."

I broke out in sweat. I swallowed my cough and left the bank thinking. *At least in America, I had some friends to help me.*

In despair, I thought of Francis, the only soul I knew in Zurich. *Would he do this? He just met me.* I called him anyway and to my surprise, he agreed to meet me at the bank right away.

After we completed the transaction, Francis asked, "Mitra, have you registered with the police?"

"Why?" I blinked back my surprise. "Do I need to?"

"Yes," Francis asserted. "Every foreign resident in Switzerland must report to the nearest police station."

I couldn't believe it. "I have a tourist visa for six months. Do I still need to?"

"Now, your plan is changed. You aren't a tourist anymore. Please do it as soon as possible."

"Will tomorrow work?" I conceded. "What time do they open?"

"Round the clock, seven days a week."

I rushed to check out of the hotel not to pay for another night.

The next day, bright and early, I walked to the police station according to Francis' direction. After filling out the necessary paperwork, an officer called me to his office.

"Lady," he announced, "you have only six weeks' permission

to stay."

"Six weeks!" I responded in a shocking voice.

"Look here."

At the Swiss embassy in Tehran, the administrator had written at the top of my visa, in tiny print: "Valid for 6 weeks."

A knot in my throat became tighter while my cough escalated. I had a hard time getting some words out. "Sir," I breathed. "everyone knows a person with a tourist visa may remain in the country for six months."

"Fraulein, not for Iranians in this time of international turmoil." The officer stood up and lit up a cigarette. "We can't accept your application. You must go back to your home country."

I had never done well with the word *must*. In a confident voice, I said, "Sir, I'm planning to register at Zurich University."

"Okay," he flicked an ash off his cigarette into an ashtray, "register there and come back with your admittance paper."

"Sir, the university is closed for the summer. I can't register until September." I held my cough in my throat.

He took another puff. "Why don't you register at a language institute?"

A small light at the end of my life tunnel, I implored, "Can I then be able to stay?"

The officer nodded, searching in the pile of papers. "Here is the list. Sign up at one of them. When you bring back the receipt, you'll get your permission to stay for the summer."

I breathed a sigh of relief. "Please tell me how to get to the first one on the list."

"We're in Oerlikon District," he explained. "Walk out of here and catch the streetcar. At Altstadt District, get off at Weinbergstrasse. It comes after 10 stops. The institute is not very far."

"Thank you so much for all your kindness, sir."

"Good luck."

On the way, I prayed they took traveler's checks. I entered the school, and this time my prayers were answered. I enrolled at the language college despite its hefty tuition of two hundred Swiss Francs for two months.

After I turned in my registration paper to the police officer, he confirmed that I could live in Switzerland for now. But that did not mean I could relax and take it easy. No steady job or income was still a huge hindrance.

As a student, I hoped that my parents would be able to send some funds. After connecting with them, they advised me to get a written permission from the Iranian Embassy in Bern, to authorize them to wire me some money.

I sent a letter right away, and two weeks later, with trembling hands, I tore open the envelope and read: "It's not possible for us to discuss your situation in writing. For clarity, an interview is needed. You must come in person to our office." My eyes filled with tears of joy when I read the rest, "No appointment is necessary."

On Monday morning, just before sunrise, I took the train bound for Bern. According to some Swiss, their capital is the most beautiful city in the world. I could not care less.

Around ten, I walked into a big, round hall. A few men and women busy typing showed no reaction, not even raising their heads.

"Salam!" I said in Farsi.

No one responded.

"Good morning," I tried again.

Still nothing.

"Guten Morgen!"

Their silence was deafening. The blood rushed to my head

when I shouted in Farsi, "Isn't this the Iranian Embassy?"

A door that until then seemed invisible, screeched, and a man with disheveled curly hair said in a somber voice, "Madam! What is the matter?"

His wrinkled, gray suit, with no tie, was less than impressive. I thought my loud voice had awakened him. He mumbled, "I'm Mr. Gilani." Then, he led me to a conference room with its bare walls. Our steps sounded as if we entered a hollow well. I handed him the letter.

He glanced at it. "Miss Tehrani, I'm very sorry to inform you that humanities are not essential areas of education for the Iranian government. Thus my hands are tied to issue permission for you to receive funds from Iran."

My angry voice filled the room, "Why didn't you explain it in the letter? I spent so much money on a train ticket and cab fare to get here." I was fuming and started coughing.

"Would you like some water?"

I shook my head.

"Madam, I can't do anything about it." Mr. Gilani shrugged. "But I would love to take you to lunch to make up for you coming all this way."

I jumped up. "No need for that, sir." I left the Iranian embassy, coughing all the way back to the train station.

After a long, exhausting day, I arrived at my flat and found the official paperwork for a change of my status in the mail. Francis informed me that by possessing the new temporary visa, I could work part-time.

"Splendid news, Francis," I said with relief, "I'll start looking for something, right away."

"But don't forget to apply to the university with no delay," he reminded me.

Yes, I'll do that tomorrow, first thing in the morning." I

transported my exhausted body to my room and closed the door.

Bright and early, I went to check with the admission office at Zurich University on my application.

"Fräulein, the requirements for an international student are," the administrator expressed, "to pass two exams, a written test in Latin, and an interview in German before you're able to register."

Surprise again caught me. "Even for a post-doctoral student?"

He nodded.

"How long do I have to prepare?"

He glanced at a wall calendar. "About seven weeks."

I held on to the counter so as not to fall down. My coughing resumed. Latin, I knew nothing about; German, I was familiar with, but not much. *What can I do?*

All night long, in my room, I pulled the shawl over my shoulders, while beseeching Reverend Mitra whose wisdom made her win the Indian Magistrate. I didn't recall getting any sleep at all. Heavey thoughts occupied my head. At one point, I realized a plan was coming to me, but no idea of its origin. I decided to put it to a test anyway.

BEFORE SUNRISE, I thought of hitting the streets, coffee shops, and subways to speak with at least fifty persons a day. I calculated that at the end of the seven weeks, I'd talk with more than two thousand people, a great practice for my German exam. A smile of triumph enveloped my face. But then I recognized one of my dragons. *I never could start a dialogue with a stranger.* Unlike in the West, in my culture, no one ever converse with a person whom we are not familiar with. I, however, ignored my *dragon*, repeated my mantra and decisively walked outside into the hustle and bustle of the city.

"*Guten Morgen! Guten Morgen!*" I said to everyone passing by me.

Some people ignored my greeting and walked by as if they were deaf. I dismissed them and kept saying, "Guten Morgen!"

Some others even looked at me as if I was a lunatic. At last, a few stopped and carried on a brief conversation after I explained my mission. They praised me for my bravery; a young woman escaped from her birth country in opposition to its dogmatic regime. These kind people lifted my soul and stirred hope in me.

Upon my early evening return, Francis, on his way to his studio asked, "How was your day?"

I sighed. "I wonder if I'll have enough practice by the end of August."

"Instead of speaking in English, we should speak in

German," Francis suggested, "so you get more practice."

"*Vielen Dank!* Thanks a bunch!" I grinned.

In my room, I picked up my Latin book and set out to my tutor's house, one street over. Upon stepping outside, Majid standing by the door shook me to my core.

"Hello, Lady Mitra." He started walking with me. "There's a gathering at my house tonight. Would you like to come over?"

"Thank you," I picked up my pace, "I have no time today."

"What time are you done?"

"I don't know." My steps became faster and faster.

"Okay. See you some other time then." He disappeared into the dark.

―◦ ⁂ ◦―

Zurich's main train station, *Hauptbahnhof*, was a shock to me during the morning rush hour. To observe this modern train station was mind-boggling. The absence of any steam or engine exhaust made the air fresh and crisp. The loudspeakers' noise blended in with the conductors' loud whistling. A crowd of men in suits, and women in skirts and jackets were moving with urgency to get to their various platforms. My black skirt and jacket with the white shirt underneath put me in harmony with them.

I chose the ticket kiosk with the shortest line. In no time my turn came up. I placed a 50 Swiss Franc note in front of the silvery man. "*Bitte.*"

The ticket agent stared at me with his weary eyes and uttered in German, "Where to?"

I answered in English. "Round trip to Geneva."

"How many?"

"One."

In a flash, he put down a ticket and my change, a bunch of bills and coins on the counter, and directed me to Platform # 2. He continued warning me in German, "Make sure not to take the train that is stopped there. It goes to Basel. Wait for the next one."

To get to my platform in my high heel shoes was a challenge as if I had forgotten how to walk. I had to be cautious so as not to slip on the smooth and spotless floor. After searching through the maze of platforms, I found the right one. While waiting for the Geneva train, I recalled the conversation I had on the phone with my American friend in Los Angeles the night before.

In an excited voice, Sharon had advised me, "Mitra, tomorrow, go to UNICEF in Geneva. With your education and the few languages you know, they would love to hire you as a translator."

"Dear, you have forgotten. I don't have permission to work."

"Don't worry," she had assured me, "when they employ you, they'll get you the permission to work too."

I was desired to land a translating job with UNICEF. However, I wished to make my way to America. Switzerland was a stepping stone. I was hoping to remain here only until the Iranian hostage crisis quelled.

I got off the cab in front of the most majestic building I'd ever seen. Its framework, made of glass, reflected its surroundings. The structure yielded to the tall trees with their bright green leaves. It looked like a mirage at first glance, a work of art, no doubt. Above the entrance door, "UNICEF" in white letters with the United Nations emblem on its royal blue awning greeted me. This oasis filled me with admiration so that all my frustration faded away.

With my head held high, I walked into the second-largest world center of "peace and love" as if I were Alice having gone down the rabbit hole. The inside of the building looked brand new, even though it was built over forty years ago. *Wow, a perfect house of glass, so fragile.* It was so quiet as if no one occupied it. The receptionist at the end of the corridor was difficult to see because of the brightness of the building.

"Hello! Where is Human Resources?" I asked, expecting to hear, *Do you have an appointment?*

The well-groomed lady, with a welcoming smile, responded, "The third floor."

Just as I turned, the receptionist walked over and pushed the button for me.

Moments later, the elevator opened, and a charming atrium appeared before me, not so cold like the Iranian Embassy in Bern. The fresh plants and flowers were a perfect accent for the beautiful green marble walls and floor. *I must have died and gone to heaven!*

"Good day," I said to a professionally dressed lady behind a desk. "I'm here to apply for a translation position."

With a kind expression, she gave me an application comprising a few pages and walked me to an empty, well-lighted conference room. "When you're done, bring it back."

I only needed to choose one language out of the three: French, German, or English. I filled in the English part, then went back to the desk.

"Thank you," the receptionist in a cheerful voice said. "The director is in a meeting now. Can you come back at two, so he can meet you?"

"Will do," I nodded. "Is there anywhere I can grab a bite to eat?"

"We have a wonderful cafeteria with excellent food." She licked her lips to corroborate, then gave me directions.

"Is it open to the public?"

"Yes, visitors are welcome."

After the elevator reached the first floor, I followed the smell of the food. Inside a large courtyard on my left, I saw a huge building inferior to the main one. It was lunchtime and several people, a mixture of men and women were in line to get their trays. I joined them too. My coughing ensued. *What can I have an allergy to in the house of peace and love?*

After lunch, I returned to the assistant's desk.

With a delighted look, she uttered, "The director looked at your application and would love to see you." She guided me to the same conference room.

To calm my nerves, I called on Reverend Mitra to give me courage.

"Hello, Ms. Tehrani." The director extended his hand. "I'm Alexandre Boucher." He sat in front of me, and in a French tempo started praising my education, then said, "Your German is not as strong as your English, is it?"

I remained quiet while looking at Mr. Boucher, a small man with a round belly and black hair. At last, I breathed out, "No sir. I'm afraid not." Then, I diverted my eyes from him.

"Too bad." He shook his head. "If your German was as good as your English I would hire you on the spot."

"How about my Persian?" I said with hope in my voice.

He shook his head again. "No, we have no need for that language."

He sounds as if Persian is an outlawed language.

I left UNICEF, the embodiment of peace and love, concluding that my entire day had been nothing but a pipe dream. *These days being Iranian is a deal-breaker.*

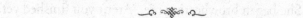

Yesterday, I lived in the world of *dreams and a house of glass*, but not today. Before sunrise, I jumped out of the bed and tiptoed to the community room. Every night, around four o'clock, Francis left the classified ads of the *Blick* newspaper on the table. Most of the wanted ads were for nannies or au pairs, with some light housekeeping. I contacted a few of them.

After calling about ten of them, their responses disappointed me. Each job had already been filled, or I had a tough time understanding the ladies' Swiss-German dialect. Three more "No" calls, then on number four, the job was still open. I perked up. The lady, Mrs. Zimmerman, asked me to come the next day and do some work for her, as a test to see how we'd like each other.

I rang the doorbell. The house was in an upper-class neighborhood. A tall, sturdy lady opened it and said, "You must be Mitra. Come in. I'm Mrs. Zimmerman." She led the way to her family room and offered me a seat.

"My two sons, seven and ten, are at school until mid-afternoon. Meanwhile, please do some dusting and ironing."

"I'd like ironing," I proclaimed.

"I have a few of my husband and sons' shirts for you to do." Mrs. Zimmerman guided me to the laundry room.

A heaps of clothes next to the set up ironing board prevented me from any reaction. I was too awestricken to reply.

Mrs. Zimmerman gestured and said, "Here they are. I'll be back in an hour to check on you. By that time, you should be ready for your next task."

She departed, leaving me in despair, but I started ironing as fast as I could.

As promised an hour on the dot later, Mrs. Zimmerman returned. She began browbeating me, "Aren't you finished yet?" She approached a rack with 15 shirts on the hangers. "Are these done?"

"Yes," I murmured.

"No. No, they can't be!" She tore one off the hanger and shoved it in my face. "Look! There are wrinkles on these collars."

I could not see any.

She threw them on the board. "For how long have you done housekeeping work?"

"Not at all," I admitted. "When I was a teenager, sometimes I ironed my father's white shirts."

"Stop! Stop! I cannot hire you!" Mrs. Zimmerman took a five Swiss Franc coin out of her pocket and handed it to me. "This is for your time and trouble. Please shut the door on your way out."

I breathed a sigh of relief and left in a search of a work that I'd good at. However, I did not know what that could be!

Soon, an interesting ad lured me: WANTED: A young woman with gorgeous hands for a dish soap commercial.

In an assuring voice on the phone, the photographer, Hermann, insisted that there would be no need for nude pictures taken of me. I thought his comment was odd. But the hefty pay of one hundred for four hours' work enticed me to make an appointment for the same afternoon.

My apprehension started boiling when I arrived at a weather-beaten building in the wall-to-wall bricked street. A couple of tipsy men were coming out of the pub on its first floor, and the strip club next door gave me a chill. My gut feeling warned me to turn around. But after reminding myself I'd have one hundred Swiss Francs in no time, I climbed the narrow, spiral stairs. A slim, dark hallway led me to the front of a scuffed wooden door. I tapped it, hoping that no one would hear.

"Come in, it's open."

I walked in. The sight of the room gave me revulsion. A tilted, lime color sofa with a broken leg occupied most of the space. In the middle, a thick black cloth attached to an outdated camera sat on a tripod. This makeshift studio also had two standing lights on each side. Before I could even decide whether to leave or stay, the grotesque, swollen face of a man appeared from behind a squalid curtain. He opened his mouth and the smell of alcohol covered the space between us.

"You must be Mitra."

I answered while trembling, "Yes."

The man walked to the sofa. "I'm Hermann."

I couldn't believe my eyes. To see Hermann in person shattered the image of him after talking on the phone. He dropped his hefty body like a ton of bricks, then relaxed into the sofa. "Dear Mitra, come and sit here." He pointed to his lap. My lack of movement made him tap on the spot next to him. "Sit here and show me your hands."

I stepped over and stood in front of him. "Look. These are my hands. I don't need to sit next to you." I extended and slowly rolled my hands to show him both sides.

"Exquisite." He reached out and held on to them. He licked his mouth like a fox. "Dear, behind the curtain, there is a robe. Change into it."

I gathered my strength and pulled my hands away and raised my voice, "Why do you want me to change? For taking pictures of my hands, there's no need for me to change."

"Yes, yes! When you are in a comfortable robe," his alcohol breath loathed me, "rather than jeans and fitted blouse, you're more relaxed."

I berated myself for being blinded by the money. On the spur of the moment, I turned toward the door, but he latched on to my arms and gave me a push toward the filthy curtain. As I disappeared behind it, my thoughts were banging inside my head. *It's okay. I'll put on the robe over my clothes.* When I looked at the pink robe, smeared with white crust and stains, it made me nauseous. I threw the robe to the floor in disgust and made a run for the door. I needed to pass by Hermann in the cramped space. And he was still reclining right there on the sofa, with a lecherous look on his face.

He must have anticipated this. As I tried to dash out, he grabbed me and got a hold of my left foot. I went down on my hands and knees. He pulled me back toward him, rising from the couch. I had little choice, and made the small sacrifice, so twisted my foot out of the shoe, which sent him reeling backward and crashing him back down on the couch.

I scrambled to my feet and rocketed out the door, not bothering to close it behind me. It wasn't easy running without a shoe, but I didn't care. The victory was mine.

Outside, the fresh air on my cheeks made my churning stomach feel at ease. I did not stop running until I'd put three blocks distance between myself and Hermann, just to be doubly safe. Then I took off my other shoe and slowed to a fast walk. I recollected what Baba Nima had said over and over: "do nothing during the day that at night when you put your head on the pillow, your inner voice prevents you from sleeping in peace."

7

A WEEK BEFORE my German and Latin exams, I received a letter from the Zurich University Admissions showing the day and time of the German test. Instead of the Latin exam, upon my admittance to the university, taking two semesters of Latin classes was enough. *Hurray, no Latin test!*

On the day of German interview, a pleasant breeze mixed with sunshine gave me a peaceful heart. Covering my shoulders with my soozany, I spent most of last night calling on the women forebears, particularly on Reverend Mitra, who saved her flock and her religion. She had to endure her sorrow being away from her beloved Persia. *Was it her wisdom to convince the Magistrate, or their collective fate made their escape a success?* I wondered.

Today, I also left my life in Fate's hand.

At ten minutes before three, I found the office. After a moment, a potential student walked out and in her blank face, "Your turn."

I stepped inside. The spacious room was dark with a ray of sunshine coming through its high ceiling, similar to a cathedral. After getting used to the dim light, in the distance I noticed a frail old man with white hair combed back, sitting on a recliner. A lamp next to him was the only light.

He looked over the black rim of his glass. In a friendly voice, he addressed me, "Fraulein, come and sit here." He pointed to an ottoman in front of him.

I did my best to stave off my rattling nerves when I greeted him, "Guten tag, Herr Professor."

"Fraulein," His friendly voice put me at ease. He continued, "do you have any family or friends here in Zurich?"

"Nein, I escaped the Ayatollah's regime."

"Why did you?" he cut me off.

"Not to abide by the new oppressive rules."

"Are you referring to wearing hijab?" he asked. "What's wrong with that?"

I hesitated.

He looked into my face. His countenance exhibited no judgment, so I spoke my mind. "I respect any woman who wears one. But Prophet Mohammad never *instructed* women to cover their heads. Now, the Khomeini regime is systematically stripping women from their individual freedom."

"Fraulein, you must be brave to seek refuge in a foreign land, all by yourself." His eyes showed admiration for me.

I responded to his following questions in confidence, carrying on as if I was talking with a long-time friend. I defended my point of view without any fear of reprisal.

"Fraulein, sehr gut, very good." A grin overtook his face, and he went on, "Your German is excellent, you have passed." He signed a form with my name on it to turn in to the registrar's office.

Hallelujah! On my way home, I bought a small box of chocolate for Francis to thank him for patiently practicing German with me.

In the flat, Agnes was watching television. "Where is Francis?"

"He's gone to his yearly military training," she answered without taking her eyes from the set.

Her reply baffled me. "Isn't he too old for the service?"

"Every year, Swiss men under the age of forty must get trained on firearms."

"But Switzerland is a neutral country, isn't it?"

Agnes shrugged. "Yes, but we must stay strong, so other countries accept our neutrality.'Armed neutrality.'" She smirked. "You have a phone message. I left it in your room."

"Thank you," I mumbled.

"U R G E NT! Call Majid. His number is," without reading the rest, I crumpled the paper and threw it into the wastebasket, wondering how he had Francis's number. I did not know who he was these days, or what he did. Like an invisible man, he watched every move I made. My heart was telling me not to trust him. But as the saying goes, *To understand a fox, one must go to his den.* I went over, dug out the paper, and dialed his number. "Is this Majid?"

"Congratulations!" he said with amusement, "You passed your exam, and now you can stay here with us."

His words sent a chill up my spine. "Who told you?"

He ignored my question and said, "Tonight, some Persian friends are coming over to my house, and you're invited too."

"Thank you, I'm busy," I said to test his resolve.

"Please," he beseeched me, "come over, meet my wife, Nasim, and my little daughter, Negar. Some other Iranian families will be here too. You'll have a good time. Do you have a pen?"

I took the bait in my mouth and wrote down his address.

A lady with a big smile opened the door. "You must be Mitra, I'm Nasim."

After hugging and kissing, she guided me to their guest room. Then she went to the kitchen.

The spacious room with its wall to wall Persian rugs, plus

crystal chandeliers, all were signs of a bountiful family. It was a mystery of what he did to afford all these in a foreign country. *He must be close to the Iranian government.*

Majid got up and introduced the only guest, a hefty gentleman, with rheumy eyes, no longer young, "This is my uncle, Hossain."

Where are the other guests? I swallowed my words.

"Lady Mitra, how long have you been in Switzerland?" Hossain asked while staring at me like a hungry wolf. He even licked his lips.

My uneasiness escalated, but before I could respond, Nasim entered the room carrying a silver tray and offered me a cup of tea and sugar cubes. Following her, a little girl with almond-shaped dark eyes and long curly hair ran in, hugged my legs, and giggled self-consciously.

"What's your name, cutie?" I asked while picking her up.

Majid answered instead, "Negar."

"She looks like an angel." I kissed her head. "How old are you?"

"She's five," Nasim responded.

Many Iranian parents will usually answer, for their child, in order to raise a "sheep" not only for her husband but for society as well.

I pressed the issue. "Dear Negar, do you speak?"

She nodded, and Majid said, "She is shy now. Give her the time, you can't shut her up."

During dinner, the smell of saffron and rosewater made my heart heavy. I could not touch the fluffy rice with lamb kabob and grilled small tomatoes. *This dinner reminds me of Maman's cooking, my home in Tehran, and my family. I felt homesick.* But I covered it well. I thought.

"Lady Mitra, how come you're not eating?" Hossain asked.

His wide smile showed his crooked yellow teeth.

Pretending I did not hear him, I continued caressing Negar's hair, who was sitting next to me.

After dinner, the two men congregated in Majid's office. I joined Nasim in the kitchen to help clean up. While washing the dishes, she pressed me, "Dear Mitra, why aren't you married?"

I glanced at her in disbelief. "Do I need a reason?"

"A young woman alone in a foreign land!" She gave me a plate to dry and continued, "Aren't you scared?"

"Scared of what?"

"Hossain is an amiable man," she offered. "He's looking for a pretty girl like you to marry."

"I hope he finds one," I said nonchalantly.

Regardless of my hint, she would not quit. "He is very well off. He has a hotel here and owns many properties in Iran."

When the tiny bird came out of the coo-coo clock and announced 9:00 PM, I broke her admiration of Hossain and rushed to say, "Oh dear, it's getting late. I have to catch the last train."

"Wait a little longer," she insisted. "Hossain has Mercedes and would love to give you a ride."

"Thank you, but no." Without waiting for her reply, or saying goodbye to Hossain and Majid, I picked up my bag and rushed out.

At the train station, I breathed freely as if I had escaped a wolf's lair. I still did not know what Majid was all about. For sure, he and Nasim wanted to marry me off to that craggy old man. No marriage for me, unless I find my soul mate. While riding the train, I recalled one of my American friends, Wendy, in Los Angeles.

I was preparing to defend my dissertation before leaving for

Iran. On an early afternoon, Wendy showed up at my place and said in her controlled, warm voice, "Mitra, I'm worried for your return to Iran in this time of uncertainty."

"Why?"

"Well," her eyes looked like a mother hen, "I don't think it's wise for you to go to the unruled land while Khomeini is in charge."

I tried very hard not to flinch and said, "I'm all ears."

She continued, "I want you to stay here and be safe."

"But dear, how?"

"Why don't you marry," Wendy urged me, "even if only on paper. By doing so, you'll get your citizenship. Then travel to Iran when the situation calms down."

I shook my head. "Marrying on paper for the sake of a green card doesn't sound right."

"Lots of people do."

"If many people are jumping out the window, does that mean I have to do the same?"

Wendy, in her kind voice, claimed, "Now is not the time for being philosophical." She smiled. "One of my friends, Peter, a student at Santa Monica College, will marry you, on paper, after I told him about your situation."

"For how much?"

She shrugged. "Go out to dinner with him and talk it over."

I murmured, "Let me think of it."

"This is his phone number. Promise you'll call." Wendy shoved a piece of paper in my hand. "Don't waste any time. Call him right away." She left me standing on a mountain of confusion. But her idea aroused my curiosity.

Peter, a slim, shy, young man, did not even look at me. Like a deer caught in headlights, he remained quiet throughout our coffee gathering

I finally said, "According to Wendy, you wouldn't mind helping me out."

He nodded. "Correct, Wendy and I want you to be safe."

"Very kind of you."

"Don't worry, Mitra. Tell me what you want me to do, and you don't have to pay me anything."

After that I knew well this was not the way an honest person dealt with her difficulties. A marriage for the wrong reason was not morally just. I thought of it deep and hard.

The next morning I called Peter. "I'm so sorry, I don't think I can go through with it. But thank you for extending a helpful hand to me."

─◦ ❧ ◦─

When I arrived home from Majid's house, it was quiet. Thankfully, Agnes was gone, so I could have some peace and quiet. I cherished my time alone. In my room, I picked up *The Centaur*, by John Updike, locked the door, and climbed into bed.

I had no idea how long I was asleep. Suddenly, the noises of some men laughing and talking loudly awakened me. At first, I thought a few drunks were passing by the window. But, the uproar escalated when their howls became clear. "Mitra! Mitra! Come out and have a drink with us." Then they murmured. After a short breaks, they started hollering again, "Mitra, don't be shy. We're Agnes's friends."

The other voice was audible. "Come out and have fun with us."

One of them even tried to open the door. I was thankful that I was cautious and had locked the door. Otherwise, one or two strangers were standing in my room. *There is no complete safe place in this world, no matter whether the East or the West.*

8

A FEW DAYS LATER, Nasim invited me to have lunch with her. I was happy to see Negar again and agreed. As soon as the host, at the Jelmoli restaurant on top of the department store, seated us, Nasim started talking, "Dear Mitra, It's wonderful that you're not returning to Iran."

"How do you know so much about me, Nasim?" I blurted out while looking at Negar.

"Don't worry." She reached for the water bottle on the table and poured some into my glass. "Majid has many friends. And we Iranians love to snoop around and get information about any new person coming to town."

I picked up my glass and bluntly asked, "What does Majid do?"

"I have good news for you," she turned a deaf ear to me and uttered. "Hossain liked you very much and would love to see if it's okay to get your father's permission to marry you."

I coughed and splattered water all over. Putting down my glass with a shaky hand, I responded, "Dear Nasim, as I mentioned before, I'm not in the market, not right now."

"Dear, unless there is something wrong with you, a beautiful young girl like you is a hot commodity in today's market." She looked at me with pity.

"What can be possibly wrong with me?"

She picked up the water glass when her right upper lip flinched. "You know what I mean."

I trembled with a rush of anger. "No, I don't."

"Like Western girls, you've already given your flower away, not to your husband."

I felt her piercing eyes on me. I could burst out of there in anger. *She considered women as 'goods', so normal in the Iranian culture.*

Without wasting a minute, or taking a breath, she continued. "Dear Mitra, how do you support yourself in this expensive land without a husband?"

"I'm looking for a part-time job."

She cut in, "Are you serious?"

"Yes, absolutely."

She looked a little stunned. "Wow, you're very Westernized."

"I guess."

During lunch, I kept busy by cutting my schnitzel into small pieces, and once in a while, I turned to Negar, smiling without saying a word. Meanwhile, Nasim babbled on about Hossain and other single male friends she and Majid had. She was only waiting for a sign of acceptance from me so that faster than I could snap my fingers, she could marry me off. At last, in order to get my attention, she said, "If you're still looking for a part-time job, there is an opening for a cashier in this department store."

"Really?"

She nodded.

"How do you know?"

She looked at her watch, yanked Negar up from her high chair, and murmured, "Go, right away, and apply. I have to run to my doctor's appointment."

"Are you all right?"

She shouted, "Yep!"

A few minutes later, I got out of the elevator and entered

the Human Resources office. The receptionist greeted me when I asked, "Do you still have an opening for a cashier job?"

She nodded and while staring at me, she carried on, "Would you like to apply?"

"Yes. May I fill out an application?"

"Great!" the lady replied. "First, our manager, Herr Schumacher will talk with you. After his approval, you'll fill out an application."

I extended my hand to the middle-aged man in a suit and tie. With a pleasant face, he offered me a seat there in his office. After some routine conversation, he asked some simple arithmetic questions. Not after long, Herr Schumacher uttered with a smile, "Very smart lady. You're hired." He then pointed to a bulky calculator machine in the corner. "Have you ever worked with this modern abacus?" He chuckled.

"No, unfortunately not," I whispered.

"No worries." He took out some bills and coins from the drawer and showed how to use the machine. In less than ten minutes, he declared, "Fraulein, go to my assistant and fill out an application. Tomorrow, come back and get your schedule for the next week."

After three days of intense training, I started at the sports section of Jelmoli and reported to its floor manager, Herr Schmidt. While transferring my tray containing some small bills and coins from the previous cashier's tray, Herr Schmidt grinned and commented, "Believe it or not, now Khomeini's son, like the Shah, has obtained a few mansions here." He let out a laugh.

I shook my head, and like a typical Iranian, did not dare to express any opinion. Besides, I refused to let my mind scatter to different places, from Switzerland to Iran, and from the present to the past. I concentrated on counting the money in the tray.

"By the way," Herr Schmidt continued, "have you been to the stores in Bahnhofstrasse?"

I looked up. "Where there are no price tags?"

He nodded.

"I'm afraid not." My nervous words jumped out. After only a few minutes on the job, and trying to learn its responsibilities, plus communicating in Swiss-German, I was in no mood to entertain my boss's hollow conversation.

"The Shah and the Empress were very good customers of them," he exclaimed.

"I can only imagine," I murmured. Then, I turned to the counter, smiled at a couple of customers in line, and greeted them, "Guten Tag."

When my shift ended, I got off at Bahnhofstrasse. Rows of shops, one after another, carried the latest fashions in clothing, shoes, and accessories. It was true, no price tag on any of them. In front of every store, there was a doorman dressed in a tuxedo. I had no business being there, a place only for the Shah and Empress to spend their nation's money. My steps became faster until I arrived at my room.

A week later, in the morning before the store opened, I was the first one to unlock the cash register. Minutes later, I was in the elevator, taking the tray from the basement to the fifth floor when it stopped on the first floor. Herr Schumacher and a polished young man stepped in.

"Good morning, Fraulein," he announced, "Herr Pachtner

meet Frauline Mitra. He's from Austria, and soon will be the director of our Jelmoli branch in Vienna."

With a smile he murmured, "Hans Pachtner."

His sharp blue eyes matched his blue tie, and his cheerful face disarmed me like a ray of light. His crisp white shirt under his royal blue suit made him look chic.

As I left the elevator, Herr Schumacher said, "Fraulein, we will make our rounds to Sporting Goods soon."

"Sounds great." I walked toward the station, unable to erase Hans's face from my mind.

A couple of hours later, Herr Shumacher and Pachtner arrived at Sporting Goods. The moment I noticed Herr Pachtner, my heart started thumping loudly. A conversation between Herr Schumacher and Schmidt got underway. Meanwhile, Herr Pachtner made his way over to me and asked, "Fraulein, how long have you been doing this job?"

"About one week."

When Herr Schumacher waved him over, he said, "It's very nice meeting you." He continued to stare at me with his eyes full of admiration. Then, he acknowledged Herr Schumacher and left.

At the end of my shift, for a change, I did not get irritated as Security searched only my bag at the exit door among other Swiss workers. I rushed and hopped on the streetcar that had stopped at the station. A few seconds later, when it started pulling away from the station, someone yelled, "Stop! Stop!"

The driver hit the break and Herr Pachtner jumped in and took a seat beside me.

I said in surprise, "Hello, Mr. Pachtner!" I was pleased to think his route was the same as mine. Our shoulders touched.

"Mitra," he whispered my name and his Austrian accent was delightful music to my ears. "We're not at work anymore. Please call me Hans," he said in practically flawless English.

"How could you remember my non-European name?"

He took out his cigarette box, lit up one, and said, "Through your file."

He looked me up. He must like me.

Hans turned his head, and our eyes met. "Tell me, I heard you lived in America for a few years."

"Who told you?"

Herr Schumacher." He looked amused. "You've made quite an impression on him."

I froze when his lips came close to my ear. "Would you like to have a drink with me? I would love to talk with you about America."

"Are you interested in going there?"

He put a hand to the side of his mouth and whispered conspiratorially, "I hope you can keep a secret. I would very much like to immigrate there one day."

"Really?" I brushed away my bangs. *Unbelievable!*

I agreed to meet him later that evening. He suggested an Irish Pub James Joyce Bar at Pelikan Strasse. I hadn't been there. It would be so exciting to go to the same bar where the author of *Dubliners* hung out, way before my time.

At the next stop, Hans got up.

"Do you live around here?"

"No, I live in the opposite way. I just wanted to talk with you." He smiled triumphantly, "see you at six." With a wink, he left.

Sooooo exciting to go out on a date. After rushing into the flat, I turned on the facet for a bath and scrubbed my bone-tired body. Then, I put on a Kashmir, v-neck red sweater with a wool-fitted black skirt, and applied some cosmetics to my face. In the mirror my appearance pleased me. Then, I wore my overcoat, high heel boots, and left.

The entrance to the Irish Pub, was a small glass door which I almost missed it. The reflection of all different bottles of booze on the gigantic mirror lighted the bar area. As soon as I saw Hans sitting at the bar, my heartbeat picked up a few paces. He'd ordered two Guinness beers and some English chips. While waiting for our drinks, he pointed to an oak table in the corner with long benches at both sides. "Do you see?"

"It used to be," the bartender drying a wine glass, came closer to us and took the words out of Hans' mouth, "James Joyce's favorite corner. He sat there for hours drinking and writing."

"Then, for a long time," Hans interjected, "that spot was for the Ulysses reading group. The members gathered every Thursday evening and had their discussions."

The bartender nodded when he put down our drinks.

"How do *you* know?" I asked Hans.

"For my English course at the college, when we had to read Ulysses, on a field trip, we came to Zurich and sat on the same spot."

I finished his thought, "And drank!"

The bartender moved closer to us and said, "Did you see that pile of dirt and building materials outside?"

We nodded.

"They'll renovate this place to be one of the most beautiful Irish Pubs in the world. One of the HSB owners bought its interior decor and furniture from Dublin."

Hans in astonishment responded, "Wow! It'd be so outstanding and authentic."

"Yes, you two need to come back and see it."

"When will it be done?" I asked.

He shrugged, "Perhaps in two or three years?"

Hans picked up his glass. "Cheers!" And stared into my eyes. "Who knows, maybe we will."

The bar atmosphere was light and airy, yet cozy and quiet —very suitable for intimate conversation. For our first date, Hans' choice of this place impressed me. I hoped some more would follow. Our one drink led to other, and we lost track of time. Occasionally, he held my hand or put his arm around me. When we kissed in front of the door to my flat, I knew for a fact there would be more dates in our future.

The following Sunday morning, while Hans and I were snuggling, the phone rang. I answered it half asleep. It was the first night he stayed over. My headache was pounding, the price of drinking too much. As far as I knew, no Iranian woman ever drank so much as to have a hangover the next day. I had become even more like a Westerner. *And I'm loving it!*

"Mitra! Are you there?"

"Yep, I'm here."

It was Layla, my younger sister in America, a student at UCLA. I gathered my words, "How are you?" I took a deep breath.

"Did you party hard last night?" She laughed. "You don't have to cover up anything from your sister.

"Maybe. What's up?" I had a tough time holding back my yawning.

"Have you heard the news?"

"No. What?"

"The Shah of Iran, the King without a country, died yesterday in Egypt," Layla said, sounding mournful.

I wiped away my tears. "Now our two-thousand-five-hundred years of monarchy is totally gone with him too."

In an excited voice, my sister went on, "Hopefully soon, the strife between America and Iran will be over, and put an end to you being stranded over there."

"Amen!" I replied automatically. I looked at Hans, realizing how much I enjoyed his company and had not thought of leaving this beautiful country either.

The news of the Shah's death left me feeling melancholy. No King, no country anymore, as if they all *puffed* into the air.

Who knows? Perhaps this is not the end of the Iranian monarchy. I consoled myself. The Crown Prince, Reza Pahlavi, could still miraculously return to Iran and free the Iranians from this despotic regime. Then, most of us staying outside the country would eagerly return to our beloved Iran.

MY LIFE BECAME routine in Zurich. Like a machine, I attended the Latin class and worked part-time. The only joy in my heart was to date Hans in secret.

At work, both of us acted formally toward each other. He was 'Herr Pachtner' and I was 'Fraulein Mitra'. After work, we transformed into secret lovers. We played our parts very well. It looked like, to be secretive ran in the Eastern and Western blood the same way. *We are all humans and are made of the same cloth.*

Hans treated me with dignity and respect. Each time he returned from Vienna, he showered me with red roses. He knew how to find the way to a woman's heart. In my innermost thoughts, I never desired to be his wife. Marriage had not been a goal in my life. Baba's voice came to my mind, "Dear Mitra, as a person, you must be financially independent before even thinking of finding a suitable man." I wondered whether I would ever meet and love a man enough to marry him.

Regardless of having Hans in my life, I had a nagging feeling on the tip of my heart to get back to America. Every few weeks, I made it my task to check with the American Consulate to find out whether they would renew my visa. Each time, as soon as I opened the door, the receptionist made a somber face and shook her head. As usual, I'd leave disappointed. It was over a year that the American hostages were still in Tehran.

In every conversation I had with Hans, he repeated, "You go, and I'll join you later."

"What if your training ends sooner?"

"You'll come with me to Vienna, won't you?" The same refreshing smile spread across his face.

"What about my classes?"

He waved a dismissive hand. "Transfer them to the University of Vienna."

"That's very farrrrrrr-fetched!"

On a bitter November day, while fixing my breakfast and listening to the news, I learned that President Jimmy Carter lost the election to Ronald Reagan. This created a ray of hope in my mind. *DING-DONG!* The doorbell interrupted my reflections.

"Salam, dear Mitra."

Nasim holding Negar's hand was standing before me. She sounded distraught. "Sorry not to call first. Could you please keep Negar for a couple of hours?"

In shock, I called for, "Is everything all right?"

"Yes," she said, clearly trying to downplay it, "I'm trying to work out some disagreements with Majid."

"I hope it's not serious."

"Negar wanted only to come to you, no one else."

I was flattered and agreed to watch her daughter. "Don't worry. Take as much time as you need."

I took Negar to the close-by park. We also had afternoon tea with our favorite French pastries in front of the fireplace in a cafe. I wondered why the desire to be a mother had never blossomed in me. Apparently, I directed my attention almost all the time to the outside world rather than to my own wishes and desires. Or may be the idea of having a family wasn't hammered into me like most other girls. I recalled Maman's words: "Dear, you do not need a husband. He won't love you as much as your father and I do." *Such a contradictory Maman I have! Sometimes she wants to have her grandchildren; but then, she discourages me to marry!*

So far, Hans had never brought up the possibility of marriage. Even though he confessed his love for me in abundance. He already had a four-year-old son. *No rush for him to have another child, and no pressure from me either.* It did not bother me at all. But I would very much like to see my dream of fleeing to America come true. And if Hans came there, then we could decide later. I refused to consider marriage as an obligatory progression of a relationship between two persons. For sure, to sign a piece of paper was not a guarantee for my happiness.

On January 20, 1981, at the inauguration of President Reagan, amazingly, right before he took the oath of office, and President Carter was no longer head of State, the Iranian students released the hostages in Tehran. Finally, my desire of continuing my passage to America blossomed in my heart once again.

In November of that year, as usual, when I visited the American Consulate, as soon as I opened the entrance door, from behind the glass window, the familiar receptionist with her hand gestured me to come inside. Only this time, with her beaming face, she declared, "Now Iranians too can travel to America."

"Do I apply for the renewal of mine?" I urged in immense excitement.

"With a good reason, yes."

"How about as a student?"

The lady nodded.

I wished I'd grow wings and could fly to my room. Upon my arrival, I threw my overcoat on the bed, rushed to the phone, and dialed Layla's number. After I explained the wonderful news to her, she responded, "The other day, I ran into your major professor on campus. He's keen to help you return to America." She breathed.

I could hear the thrill of going back to America in my voice. "Please, please, appeal to him for an admission form."

"Will do! Are you in a rush to come over?"

"Yes, I want to taste the triumph between my teeth sooner than later."

~ ❦ ~

Within a few weeks, I received my admission form and bolted to the American Consulate. After filling out the heaps of pages again, she left me in the same room where I had waited over a year ago. The only difference was, President Reagan's picture had replaced President Carter's.

Before even sitting, the door opened, and I recognized the Consul, James Herald. I felt a chill take over my body, expecting the same former result. To my surprise, he extended his hand for a handshake, and said with a grin, "Dr. Tehrani, have a seat."

Unbelievable. A year ago, he treated me like dirt. I concentrated on the present.

"Would you like something to drink?"

"No, thank you," I replied, still not completely convinced.

He surprised me when he sat in the chair next to me, not behind his desk.

"Khomeini is quite old, isn't he?"

His opening question took aback me. "Yes."

"How old is he? Do you know?"

"Very old, in his eighties or nineties." I tried to cover my pounding heart with a smile, wondering where he was going with his questions.

"Who do you expect will replace him?" Mr. Herald inquired. "Do you see perhaps his oldest son?"

"There is a so-called 'president' elected for six years." I shrugged. "Khomeini is officially a Supreme Leader."

"How do you like his administration ?"

"I escaped that dictatorship."

"And especially its bias toward women," Mr. Herald completed my view.

I nodded.

The Consul went on, "I have one more question."

"I'm all ears."

"How do I know you will not stay in America permanently once I renew your visa?"

I smiled. "Sir, you are asking me to predict the future. I am no fortune teller and have no crystal ball before me. I'm a scholar eager to continue my research on my favorite American author and possibly publish it."

Mr. Herald started laughing and got up. "Dr. Tehrani, come tomorrow and get your new visa. It is in your best interest to go back to the United States."

After thanking him, I flew outside as if I had received my wings. My heart was filled to the rim with both joy and sorrow. I hadn't really thought about it till this very moment. But to leave behind my dear new friends made my eyes tear up.

~⚬~❖~⚬~

On the plane, I notice: Yes; I was overjoyed to be flying to the country that I considered my second home. However, a load of sorrows weighed me down. *Why do I have to leave Hans, and beautiful little Negar?* The ones I kept close to my heart. It had to be my fate to be separated from my family in Tehran, and now from my friends in Zurich. It baffled me how strongly Baba believed in fate. There was no confusion for him. I remembered when I asked him once in Tehran, "Baba, is it my fate to drink this glass of water in front of me?"

"My dear, it is your *fate* if you drink it, and it is your *fate* if you don't."

"So, we're predestined."

"Absolutely. Fate is a catalyst for shaping our lives."

"Some claim it a chance event, don't they?"

Baba nodded, looked into my eyes. "My dear, we refuse to admit an invisible force in our life which really controls the events."

How come, most Easterners believe in fate, but Westerners are convinced they are in charge of their own destiny?

I glanced out the window to calm my mind. To fly above the clouds at an amazing speed, did not seem we were moving. Was it possible that we do not see the hand of Fate, so we do not believe it?

Then, like a bird, my thought flew to Hans. I admitted my love for him, however, it was not quite strong enough to let me ignore my desire. Otherwise, I would've pushed aside my dream of going to America. The scene at the Zurich airport, saying goodbye to him, flashed before my eyes. His sadness was obvious in his face. He whispered in my ear, "Darling, you have too much stuff."

"Agreed. An enormous suitcase, two bags of books and my

two volume-dissertations, *From Land of Roses and Nightingales*, which I have to carry in my hands. ”

"Why don't you leave them with me?" He offered a reassuring smile. "I'm coming as quickly as you've settled."

"Are you sure?"

"Of course," he raised his right hand from my waist, held it up as a sign of swearing, and said, "I vow to take good care of them."

I kissed him. "Thank you. They are my *children*."

"I'm quite aware of it." He enveloped me in his arms and hugged me like there was no tomorrow.

God knows how long it'll be until I see him again.

To leave Negar was difficult too. Each time I picked her up and felt the warmth of her little body against my chest, my heart soared.

The nine-hour flight from Zurich to New York went by in the blink of an eye. We passed over the Statute of Liberty while the plane descended to land. I stretched to hug this 'Lady of Liberty'. As a dignified woman, I also stood to the dictatorial regime, and followed other women before me, and chose a path to freedom.

10

UPON MY ARRIVAL at JFK Airport in the early afternoon, like a sheep ready to be immolated, I followed the crowd to the American Immigration and Customs Office. My student visa to continue my research at UCLA was adequate for letting me into the country. But, I could not explain my bewilderment. I have come so near, yet so far.

The line moved slower than a snail. Even the next minute of the future was unknown. The word "NEXT," shattered my anxious being.

I placed my passport in front of the officer. The moment he gazed at its maroon color, he shot me a bleak look, picked it up, opened it, and hand-signaled another nearby officer. She walked into the glass booth. They gazed at my passport and talked under their breaths. The second officer raised her head and looked at me. "Madam, come with me."

I had to pick up my pace to catch up with her. Almost out of breath, I uttered, "Officer, is there a problem?"

When there was no response, I understood she did not wish to reply until we were in a private room. Maintaining her silence the entire lengthy walk was like sprinkling salt on my nerves. At last, she stopped before a door, unlocked it, and gestured for me to enter. "Have a seat until I come to get you."

I knew well, if they denied my entry, they would send me

back to Iran, the last place on earth I wanted to go. My coughing and churning stomach came over me. At this moment, there was nothing else to do except to sit and abide by the hand of Fate.

I looked around the room where I sat on a bench. It had a frosted glass wall connected to another office. At the end of the second one, a full-size window displayed the landscape of the Big Apple. The sunset on the horizon, and the rows of skyscrapers, with the miniature looking colorful cars and trucks, would make a memorable postcard.

In a short time, the darkness started diminishing my sight; and soon after, an officer entered the adjunct room. Oblivious to me, he switched on a bright desk lamp and looked through my passport. He was validating its authenticity as if it were a diamond. At long last, he turned off the light. His steps pounded in my head. I continued waiting and refused to look at my watch. Time had no meaning. By now, I had missed my connection to LA. Not to mention the gnawing hunger and thirst. My life was on hold.

I jumped up when the door banged open. In the dim light of the room, I fixed my eyes on the new officer's lips.

"You can go now." He handed me my passport and continued, "The airline has your luggage. Check to see what time your next connecting flight is."

"Thank you, sir." I breathed a heavy sigh of relief. "Thank you, sir."

My elation was beyond measure. Like a bird freed from the cage, I ran to Pan Am's booth and found no one, no sign of the previous horde as if they all had vanished. A blank monitor only showed "10 PM". I collapsed on a seat right before the counter after giving up looking for something to eat or drink. I opened my passport and stared at the seal of the entry to America. It wiped away all my anguish.

A harsh voice startled me. "Hey! Don't you know the airport is closed?" He was a security guard.

I nodded and could barely get the words out, "I missed my connection."

After staring at me for a moment, he said, "Lady, didn't you hear me? No one may stay here through the night."

"I know!" The words narrowly skipped my lips.

"Well," he responded while his right foot tapping the ground. "This means you must get out."

I moaned. "I don't have anywhere to go."

He raised his voice, "Not an excuse." He pushed his jet-black hair under his cap. "Go to a hotel."

In my boned tired voice, I uttered, "I don't know any."

"Get out!" He demanded and his anger was obvious.

I stood up. "Okay, okay."

When he saw I would comply, he calmed down a little and offered, "Outside, catch a cab and tell him to take you to the Ramada Inn."

When checking in, I asked if they had a restaurant inside.

"Yes, we do." The receptionist in his sleepy eyes said. "It's closed. There is a Bob's Big Boy two blocks away."

Not safe to walk all by myself this late at night, not in America. Perhaps I would've done it in Europe.

That short night, after calling Layla and letting her know I was staying in the Big Apple, I laid on the bed. Excitement kept me from sleeping, just counting the minutes.

The next morning, before sunrise, I collapsed on a chair by the Pan Am ticket counter and dozed off. A clickety-clack of shoes forced me to open my eyes. A woman and a man dressed in their uniforms got busy opening the booth. I leaped over. "Good morning, where can I get a connection flight and locate my luggage?"

Looking at me with her sharp eyes, she answered, "Your passport, please."

I put it in front of her.

After she compared me with the picture in the passport, she said in a kind voice, "We don't keep any luggage here. Apparently, it went to Los Angeles on the flight without you."

The other ticket agent came closer to the counter. "Why did you miss your connection?"

I covered my nervousness with a smile and replied, "It took forever to clear customs."

In no time, the lady issued my boarding pass and instructed me how to get to the departure gate. After almost two years, I would once again see Layla and my L.A. friends. I adhered to Rumi's saying: *Set your life on fire and seek those who fan your flames.* During my previous studies in America, I had accumulated quite a few of them. They were all waiting to welcome this Easterner who had achieved her goal of finding freedom.

In Los Angeles, I lived with Layla while putting all my efforts into finding employment and obtaining my permanent residency. One day, I received a call from Janet, a friend from my humanity class at UCLA. She worked for the federal government and was eager to help me build up a path to stability. "I've heard the American government is looking for a few translators."

"Do you know if Farsi is one of them?" In a skeptical voice,

I carried on, "I don't want to be disappointed as I was in Geneva."

"Don't be cynical," she said in her usual bright voice, "knock on several doors until one opens."

I exaggerated my exhaustion. "I'm too tired of knocking."

"Mitra, you've climbed a huge mountain. Don't stop now." Janet's tender words were clear. "In Rome, do as Romans do," she giggled. "It takes only a phone call to find out."

The same night, I set the alarm clock to make an early call to Washington, DC, first thing the next morning. After several tries, an HR officer said, "Yes, we do need translators for Farsi." The lady promised to put a package with an application and other materials in the mail.

To my surprise, I received heaps of necessary paperwork within ten days. Besides the application, there were several pages to translate from Farsi to English and vice versa. The three books to read surprised me the most: *From the Shadows, Inside the Company,* and *The Spy's Bedside Book.* They were part of the preparation for the interview if I passed the written exam.

─〜❦〜─

A couple of weeks later, after mailing everything, I took the best phone call in my life.

"Dr. Tehrani?" The lady's voice was dry and formal.

"Speaking," I said hesitantly.

"Regarding the application, you sent us. Congratulations, you passed the written part."

I had no idea how to control the butterflies in my stomach. Within two weeks I was on a plane to DC, one of my favorite capitals in the world.

The following day, after checking out of the hotel, a cab

dropped me off at the designated address. I stood in front of a nondescript brick building amongst tall red maple trees, birches, and old oaks. All their yellow and red leaves carpeting the ground set forth the arrival of fall. There was no name on the front; Just a number: 3055. The tinted windows prevented me from seeing inside. My suspicion arose. I checked the number again and in a hesitant way entered.

The small reception area was quiet, except with two security guards behind a seven-foot-tall glass shield. One of them asked me to find my name and sign in front of it. After checking my ID, he instructed me to walk with my suitcase through a scanner similar to the ones at airports.

He took a hold of my suitcase and said, "Please go to the third floor. They're waiting for you."

In the elevator, my cough returned. Instead of getting angry, I thoughtfully recited my mantra, *By connecting my brain, heart, and hands, I create a unity able to heal, awaken and liberate all I am. Then, I realized, I am the Master of my destiny.*

When the elevator door opened, the sight of a prim and proper lady in a business suit put my turbulence at ease. She greeted me warmly and escorted me to a conference room. She left after closing the door behind her.

Despite no windows, the florescent fixtures above lit the room well. A rectangular table in the middle with eight chairs filled almost the entire space. The seven plain looking people were engaging in a lively discussion. As soon as I sat in the last one, the five men and two women, stopped talking and turned to me.

To answer their wide curious eyes, I readily responded, "I'm Mitra."

When I raised my head, a tiny camera in a corner near the ceiling shocked me. *Wow!* They were taping us.

Soon, two middle-aged ladies dressed like homemakers in colorful outfits and high heel shoes walked in with gigantic smiles and started their presentation. They explained some details about the organization with the emphasis on how covert our jobs would be. For the married applicants, their spouses were subject to clearance as well. And the ones who wished to marry after their employment had to get the bureau's permission first.

At the end, they handed each one of us a piece of paper with the room number where we needed to report. Down the hall, I found room #3, opened the door, and walked in. It looked like the interrogation room at a police station. There was one desk with two chairs opposite each other. I refused to sit down and started pacing.

After about 15 minutes, a man in a black suit entered, wearing a CIA badge on a lanyard around his neck. He introduced himself as Agent Wilson gestured for me to sit, and then he took the seat opposite me. He asked, "Miss Tehrani, would you like to have some water or coffee?"

"No, thank you." I was too nervous to have anything.

Agent Wilson in his dry and formal voice, said they had selected me as one of a few candidates for a special assignment because of my knowledge of Farsi; and my relationship to a "party of interest".

"Miss Tehrani, if this interview goes well, and you accept our offer," he looked into my eyes and continued, "We will employ you for about a year, and paid handsomely." He opened the folder in front of him. Then, he raised his head. "Let me be clear. *You*, Miss Tehrani, *will not* be on record as an employee of the CIA. Rather, you'll be an independent contractor. Your documentation will look 100 percent legitimate and show that you are working for an import/export company in Boston. That is your cover."

My mind was racing. *Who is that person of interest? Do they want me to be a spy? I don't see myself leading a double life. What would Reverend Mitra do? Why has our modern time made life so complicated? Totally baff...*

Agent Wilson's voice interrupted my thoughts, "Well, what do you say?"

"Can I think about it?" I breathed out.

"Right now, is all you have." He stared at me and waited for a reply.

I had no idea how to calm myself. In an instant, I decided this job or assignment was not for me. As soon as I started to get up, and say *No, thank you.* I heard Agent Wilson.

"I believe you do know Majid Enayati."

To hear his name shocked me to my core and in a slow motion sat back down. "Y-Yes. What exactly do you want from me?"

"You are to translate the letters written by Majid, who is living in Boston now." He stopped and searched into my eyes. "It's possible some fieldwork involved."

"Fieldwork? What does that mean?"

The Agent replied, "If the letters do not provide sufficient evidence to arrest Majid for his alleged crimes, we need you to engage him in person, and have one or more conversations with him. And if this is the case, you wear a wire."

Here comes Majid into my life again. I was disgusted.

"Sir, this task sounds very dangerous." I wiped my forehead.

Agent Wilson with the same formal voice replied, "There will always be an agent in your vicinity for your safety like your shadow. You will never see him or her. There will also be a code word. If you find your life is in imminent danger and you say it, the agent will come to your aid. But I must advise you, once this happens, you have compromised the mission. Of course, we would not like this to happen."

Oh, my gosh, this job is getting riskier by the minute.
Everything inside of me was telling me not to take the offer. *Get out of here, and never look back.*

The Agent's voice broke the silence. "In all events, once the mission is complete, so is your employment with us are done. However, we will then find you a new, legitimate job to your liking in one of the three cities of your choosing: New York, Chicago, or DC."

"With this new offer, can I think at least overnight and give you my answer tomorrow morning?" I beseeched him.

He shook his head. "Now or never."

To do anything in haste, or to accept a job on the spot was always a *no-no*. While I was not sure to take the assignment, as if Agent Wilson read my mind, he pushed a picture in front of me. The photo was somewhat grainy. I couldn't believe my eyes when I stared at it. It was Ben, handcuffed and being led away by a couple of Iranian police officers in Tehran airport. Drums beat in my head, drums of remembered pain.

With tearful eyes, I asked, "Why are you showing me this?"

"We don't have proof." He paused. "That's why we need you. We believe Majid set Ben up. The Iranian government recalled Ben back to Tehran. The trap was ready for him." He hesitated a moment. "You know what happened next."

I nodded and wiped my tears. *Ben was an innocent man caught in the web of a devil.* After a long silence, and pulling myself together, I said, "I'll do it."

"Good." Agent Wilson's voice became softer, "Now, before you sign these confidentiality papers, let me emphasize. You must swear to the secrecy of this assignment. Never, ever divulge it to anyone, not even your sister."

They know everything about me. I replied, "Understood." Then I started signing the papers.

After finishing, I got up, and the Agent extended his hand and said, "The clearance will take some time. Be patient."

I left the Bureau with mixed emotion, wondering if my assignment was as safe as Agent Wilson had made it sound.

~◦11◦~

1983

THE SOUL OF AMERICA, Boston, the high-minded city, became my new temporary hometown. I came out of the long background check in the clear and received my employment papers as a "translator" with Trade House an import-export company.

I hoped Majid would not be the same person as the CIA is looking for. It was not unlikely to find two or three people with the same name. The man I was familiar with couldn't possibly have a dark heart causing Ben's death. He was a kind family man. But if he was the one, could he turn his innocent daughter, Negar, into a monster like himself? *No way!* I continued wondering.

After a couple of weeks on the job, I received a hefty packet with a red stamp of "CONFIDENTIAL" on it. The letters in Farsi signed by *M. Enayati,* attached to it a picture of a man with a scar on his left cheek, shook me to my core.

A note from Agent Wilson instructed me to contact Majid and revive the old friendship. I had to pretend that my running into him was incidental. It provided his home address and phone number. I sank deep into thoughts of Negar's long curly hair and Nasim's worried eyes.

"Mitra?" An assistant, Mary, in her low-cut red blouse, standing before my cubical, broke my concentration. "Have you been to the pub, Cheers, yet?"

"Nope."

"After work, the girls are going there," she said. "Why don't you join us?"

Still spellbound by the packet, I responded, "I don't think so."

"After five days work," Georgina, in her tight sexy blue jeans, from her desk, in a whisper-shout said, "Don't we deserve a Happy Hour?"

Mary laughed. "Who knows, perhaps you'll meet your Prince in Shinning Armor?"

I replied with certainty, "I'm not looking for one."

"Come on," Georgina insisted, "every woman is waiting for one."

Then all of them burst out laughing.

"I told my finance', Tom, to come with us." Kathy who had a voluptuous bosom spoke up. "When a guy accompanies a bunch of girls, the other men become courageous and approach the single girls in a hurry."

The girls did not take no for an answer. So, I shoved the papers in the desk drawer, locked it, picked up my purse, and followed them like a sheep.

After walking down into a place filled with smoke and wall-to-wall people, we reached the bar by some pushing and shoving. Mary, the closest one to the bartender, ordered our drinks over the ones sitting on the stools. The band on the other side was playing a deafening Rock and Roll tune. As soon as soft music filled the space, a man asked Mary to dance; and right after that Georgina was also on the dance floor. Kathy and Tom joined the crowd on the stage. Busy with my thoughts, I looked down, expecting no one to invite me to boogie.

When several men bumped into me to get closer to the bar, I stepped toward the exit door and stood in a corner. It'd be so long until Monday morning. I wished Hans was with me. *Ah, just a dream. Why does my mind still fly to him? I must forget him.*

Our phone calls and letters had stopped. The last conversation I had with him I still lived in Los Angeles.

"Dear Mitra," Hans' jolly voice sounded in my ear, "I'm done with my training in Zurich, and I am the manager of one of the Jelmoli stores in Vienna."

"Great, now you're the big boss," I said. "Are you still interested to come to America?"

"Let's see what happens," he replied in a voice void of encouragement. "My son's mother and I are thinking to patch up the relationship between us."

Not long after that call, I found a heavy airmail package sitting at my front door. My precious books, the ones he insisted I leave with him, and he would bring them to me when he'd come. No note accompanied them. For sure, Hans had nailed the coffin well.

Now, in Cheers, I dismissed my thoughts of flying to him. To be an independent person satisfied me. I accepted my fate to live alone for the rest of my life.

"Would you like to dance?" A man's whisper to my left ear interfered with my thoughts.

"No thanks," I replied without turning to look at him.

Other men, when I rejected them, would leave. But not this one. He remained standing beside me. After a moment, he inquired, "Are you with the bride or groom?"

The sound of my laughter surprised me.

The guy, now standing in front of me, caught my attention. A few wrinkles around his eyes were signs of him being a few years older than me. He stood taller than me in my high heel shoes. His black tailored pants, white shirt under his black jacket without a tie, signaled he had to be a businessman of some sort, and coming from his office. His dark clean-cut hair showed his handsome face very well.

"I'm Robert."

"I'm Mitra." I allowed him a small smile.

"You must be Persian," he said matter-of-factly.

His top lip was thin, but his full bottom lip and cleft chin melted away my resistance. In amazement, I asked, "You're right. How do you know?"

He inched closer to me. "At Boston University we had several students from Persia in the late sixties."

"What do you do, Robert?"

"I'm a civil engineer." He lifted an eyebrow. "Do you know what that is?"

With a smile, I responded, "Of course, I do."

"I thought in your country you still ride camels." The corner of his lips flinched.

With a wide smile, I responded, "Of course, every day my father takes his camel to the office in his three-piece suit."

He roared with laughter.

I saw Georgina approaching me with worry in her eyes. "Here you are! I've been looking for you everywhere."

"I'm here." I uttered.

"I thought you'd left already," Georgina said in a tipsy voice. "Are you ready to go?"

"Yes," I said, although not so antsy to leave anymore.

Can I call you sometime?" Robert inquired.

I whispered my number to him, confident that he wouldn't remember. Then, I proceeded outside with Georgina.

"Where is Mary?" I asked.

Georgina chuckled. "Oh, she'll get a ride home later."

All night, thoughts of Majid haunted me. How to reconnect with him was a puzzle difficult to solve. Then the chain of my thoughts took me to Tehran, and my dashing tutor, Bijan. I'd had a vigorous crush on him as a teenager.

~❀12❀~

I COMPLETED my last high school test. According to my
parents, time was of the essence, and I had to work right away
on the university entrance exam. They hired a tutor, Bijan, the
younger brother of one of Maman's friends. Recently, he had
received his doctorate degree from Tehran University in
chemical engineering. He had to be an *Übermensch*, superman.

On the first day, after ironing out his fee, Baba called me to
our home library with a small round table and three chairs. As
a gentleman, Bijan stood up and shook hands with me. His
beige sports jacket and dark brown trousers looked stylish. His
black short hair parted on the side and combed away from his
face, showing his amazing hazel eyes. When Baba left the room,
he put the lesson plan on the table. "Mitra, such an unusual
name you have."

"Really?"

"Do you know what it means?"

I looked into his eyes and said, "Light."

"You shine like a light." He stared into my eyes, "In
Zoroastrianism, *Mitra* is also a symbol of the Sun."

I confirmed it with a nod, continuing to gaze into his eyes,
searching for some warm feelings, but to no avail. His eyes
weren't talking to me. *Why not?*

I admit my life was sheltered. I knew nothing of the

opposite sex. I did not even have a brother. Jahan had died from pneumonia when I was around three years old. Besides, in Iranian society co-education did not exist. When the Shah intended to put an end to the segregation of children, the opposition voices of the clergymen stood in his way. This part of modernization never took off the ground in Iran. Girls and boys were raised not to talk openly with each other unless they were part of their clans. However, in my case it was different.

One year before I reached the school-age of seven to be eligible to start my first grade, Maman decided it was time for me to sit in her first-grade class, so I would be an outstanding student of the following year.

She was determined to teach at an all-boys school, for she believed lads were smarter than maidens. I recalled the first day I went with her. After a long bus ride, we got out at the far east of Toopkhaneh Square. The hustle and bustle in the street made Maman hold on to my hand tight so when the crowd were rushing and elbowing me, I wouldn't fall down. Then, while we were passing by huge, majestic buildings, Maman pointed out: "Dear Mitra, this building with four narrow marble columns is called, the Palace of Justice."

I made a gesture to each side of the building. "What are those statues?"

"Dear, on the right is our King Cyrus the Great. He was famous for being benevolent to the victims of slavery."

"What about the other one?" I called her attention to. "The man with two wings upon his back."

"Dear, he is the Angel of Justice in full armor. He carries a scale on one hand and on the other a sword pointing down toward the people bowing, or kissing his feet."

I was in awe. "But why?"

"It means that justice has to have a scale to measure the

punishment to fit the crime, and to have the power to rule against anyone who commits a crime."

"But a helmet covers his face. How could he rule?"

"That is the whole idea. He can't see to like or dislike a perpetrator, or an innocent person. His ruling is based on the body of proof, and he has to be impartial."

"Maman, I love the mosque ahead of us. Its blue dome is awesome."

"Yes, dear, this mosque is so majestic that it's called 'The Shah Mosque'."

"Does our king come here to pray?"

"In the past, they did. But not now." She then looked to our right. "This building with arches and mosaic work on its walls and a few stairs is our Parliament."

"What is a Parliament?"

"It's where the people's representatives make the laws for our land."

Its darkness bothered me. "Why does it have no lights?"

Maman's voice became sad when she whispered, "It's locked. His Majesty decides when to open it."

"What is the next building with the winged lions etched in the stones?"

Her voice picked up proudly. "Dear, that is the largest museum in Iran. It's full of artifacts from ancient times, and modern arts. We can even find King Cyrus' decrees, the first proclamation on human rights on display."

"Is the Shah as benevolent as King Cyrus?"

Maman grumbled. "He's trying."

As soon as she and I entered the school, the bell rang. We continued our short walk to the classroom. About 40 boys in their gray uniforms, each with a white collar, stood up for us. The scene was stunning. I felt like royalty

My mother said. "Have a seat!"

Everyone scrambled for a seat.

"Mitra dear," she whispered in my ear, "sit anywhere you would like." Maman let go of my hand and climbed the three steps toward her wooden elevated desk and chair. On her right, a huge blackboard held pieces of chalk and a dark black eraser on its edge. The massive classroom was well lit with four huge high-up windows so the students could not see out of them.

The boys' childish voices jarred my ears. The ones sitting at the end of each bench pushed the other three toward the wall to make room, tapping on the space, "Come! Come! Sit here."

"No, no! Here!"

I looked around. In the first row, the boy at the end was quiet, and there was an empty spot beside him. I was their *queen* and chose my spot.

As I sat down, I heard my mother say, "Okay boys, be quiet!"

All of a sudden the clatter stopped.

Every day I had fun; especially when I could read the alphabet on the board, or from our book, before any of the boys. Or, I was the only one raising my hand to answer a question.

After a few weeks, the boys asked my mother if I could go out with them during the recess. On the playground, some of the boys pushed me, but there were always a few to rescue me. In those days, I learned some of them could run much faster than I could.

The following year, when I went to the girls' school in our neighborhood, the days at boys' school became like a dream. Among the girls, I was no longer special. The older ones made fun of me or bullied me. With the first snow in Tehran, I wore my overcoat made of sheepskin.

During the break, a few of them in fifth or sixth grade held me and screamed, "Hey, Zahra! Today, we have a lamb with some patches of black."

Then, Zahra, in her long face with mean eyes, stepped toward me and smacked me on the head. "Great, this one is perfect for sacrifice. Then we feed her meat to the neighborhood dogs."

Even though I was afraid, I held back my tears. I could not possibly get away either. The other girls circled around me and Zahra. So I stayed quiet while she picked on the knots of the coat, and pushed me while the other girls shouted, "Harder! Harder!"

I poured all my strength into my feet so as not to fall down, regardless of how hard she hit me. That afternoon, as soon as I arrived home, and Maman saw my wet eyes, she bought me an overcoat similar to the other girls'.

In high school, the girls behaved much nicer. They were busy focusing on how to communicate with a boy or when they would get married. They satisfied their curiosities about them by having conversations with each other. They could only be next to them, or meet them while walking to and from school.

Interestingly, some of the girls whose family obligated them to cover their hair, after a few steps away from school, took their hijab off, and shoved it into their bags. Most of them had long braided hair. No one wore it loose. The sight of a woman's hair excites sexual fantasies in men, according to some mullahs. And it would be her sin not to hide it under the scarf. It pleased me that my hair was almost as short as boys'. My mother did not have time to fiddle with it. In high school, however, I could have long hair, at shoulder length.

In the tenth grade, I respected my literature teacher, Ms. Mehrab. Some of my classmates felt sorry for her. She had to be in her late thirties and single, a distressful subject for them.

Nonstop, they talked about her, especially Batool. She said, "For sure, she'll be a spinster for the rest of her life. Her prime time for a suitor is long gone." Most of the students repeated their frustration right before she entered the classroom.

Ms. Mehrab was the only single female teacher we had. In high school, we did have one or two male instructors too. They wore rings. No single ones instructed in our high school.

One day, a bunch of girls started whispering to each other while Ms. Mehrab was reading one of Rumi's poems:

In your light I learn how to love.
In your beauty, how to make poems.
You dance inside my...

She stopped. Her kind voice was always assuring. "Hey, ladies, what's going on?" She never raised her voice to us despite the room sounding like a swarm of bees.

"Ms. Mehrab," Zari called out, "Fati's saying we must pray for you to marry soon."

"How do you know I'm not married?" Ms. Mehrab challenged.

"It's easy," Sima injected, "your eyebrows aren't plucked."

Then Sakineh chimed in, "And you're not wearing a ring."

With a gentle smile, Ms. Mehrab uttered, "It's clear. Your *bodies* are here, but your minds are far, far away."

We all burst out laughing.

Tooba grumbled from the last row, "Ms. Mehrab, don't you have any suitors?"

The irony in Ms. Mehrab's voice was clear. "Not really. Most men would like their brides to be young and fresh. Younger girls are easier to bend, like a twig. And they barely ever break." She kept her smile and under her breath, she continued, "I guess

I'm too old, or too smart for any man."

I wondered, *Shouldn't women fall in love and marry too?*

Khadijah, sitting next to me said. "If it weren't because of His Majesty changing the old Islamic rule of the girls to marry at age nine, and boys at age 16, by now, we would've very likely had at least a few kids."

Ms. Mehrab nodded. "Please, keep in mind, before Islam, in Arabia, some poor fathers considered having a girl was a burden. So they buried their daughters alive."

I repeated what I had heard over and over from my father. "His Majesty isn't the only one liberating women. Our Prophet Mohammad gave respect to women in Arabia in the seventh century."

"Correct, Mitra." Ms. Mehrab nodded and went on. "The prophet came up with this rule of marriage to respect and celebrate women. He did not mean they had to consummate the marriage. Usually, the groom's family took the girl to their house and the mother-in-law trained her according to her family tradition."

"It's still the same way among my relatives," Fati exclaimed. As she covered a wisp of hair under her scarf, she continued with a smile. "Every girl must get married, according to our mullahs."

Ms. Mehrab closed her book. "Today, your mind is not with Rumi. I'll bet you're thinking he refers to the passionate love, the same feelings boiling inside each one of you."

A heavy silence blanketed the entire classroom. One of the bravest, Zobeideh murmured, "Clearly, he's talking about his lover, a woman, isn't he?"

"Do you think Rumi had nothing else to write except about his beloved?"

Most of us came into one voice, "Who else?"

Ms. Mehrab questioned. "Have you not heard of the Ultimate Love?"

None of us breathed a word and looked at each other like lost souls until we heard Ms. Mehrab again: "God Almighty, my children," her excited voice filled the room, "Rumi was a Sufi, believing the only love worthy in life is the Love of Deity."

Some students smirked when Fati blurted, "Ms. Mehrab, I'm not allowed to read Rumi at home. He wasn't a Moslem."

"I'm sorry." A cloud of sorrow came over our teacher's face. "Rumi was the unique Moslem in the world." She brushed away her hair from her forehead. "This is how our system brainwashes our young ones. They know nothing about our geniuses." She paused. "Our autocratic regime keeps pushing us to the abyss of ignorance, instead of educating our minds. Isn't it easier to rule over indigents than elites?"

A heavy silence covered the room.

"Is that the reason," I asked in confusion, "some of our young ones go to the West to study, and never return home?"

"Very likely, Mitra." Ms. Mehrab looked astonished. "In their societies, the road of learning is open for anyone who would like to walk the path of education." She then stepped closer to us and continued, "Let's be friends, so I can talk bluntly with you all."

"Hurray!" We cheered and closed our books.

"I hate to say this about our culture," Ms. Mehrab's voice became serious, "regardless of modernism, our nation is still dragging itself blindfolded behind the Western countries."

"But it wasn't this way in Persia during ancient times, was it?" I questioned.

Ms. Mehrab lowered her voice. "You're right, Mitra." She then paused as if debating to verbalize what it was in her heart. "You know that we, Persians, had our own monotheistic religion, Zoroastrianism. It is baffling that how the Arabs were successful in the conquest of the mighty Persian Empire. When our king becomes corrupted and can only think of his own welfare rather than the people's…" Ms. Mehrab stopped. After she took a deep breath, she looked directly into our eyes. "Westerners have the freedom of speech, my children." She paused while heavy clouds of sadness covered her face. "Let me tell you the reason I'm not married."

We all listened with rapt attention when she explained, "In our culture, as you know, we separate girls from boys, ignoring their curiosity about each other. None of us know anything about the opposite sex, except talking with our friends, as ignorant as we are. Then, under the name of marriage, one night, a girl must do the most intimate action with her so-called 'husband' who is nothing more than a stranger to her." Ms. Mehrab swallowed hard. "And if she refuses to obey, or show no bloody handkerchief to her in-laws, in some cases, she would end up with a black and blue body."

In a sad voice Zahra followed Ms. Mehrab's thought, "In my village, I remember one time a woman accused of adultery got killed for all the stones that the residents threw at her."

Ms. Mehrab's eyes became teary. "This is a barbarian tradition," while wiping her eyes, she continued, "this only stains our culture and Islam." She swallowed hard and went on, "There is absolutely no evidence that Prophet Mohammad instructed this kind of punishment for a woman."

"Ms. Mehrab, how could you escape any of these?" Zari asked boldly.

She shook her head. "I put my foot down that I wouldn't marry unless I felt comfortable being with my future husband."

"And your father agrees." Fati murmured.

"When I was ten years old," Ms. Mehrab uttered, "my

father passed on, and there was no brother to interfere with my life either. I guess I'm the lucky one." She winked and smiled.

At the sound of the bell, Ms. Mehrab wished all of us the best of luck and left.

‑◦❦◦‑

During the days, while waiting for my time with Bijan, I daydreamed of the movie, *To Sir, With Love*. It showed a high school in England, and their handsome teacher, Sidney Poitier. He must deal with a group of untamed students, especially the one with long blonde hair who has a crush on him. She does whatever she can to get him to pay attention to her.

It disappointed me when she did not get married to him. If that movie would portray an Iranian high school, there would be no boys in the classroom. The students would have no blonde hair or makeup on. And if a girl believed she was in love with the teacher, she'd show her puppy love for him with non-verbal communications. And no one else would be aware of her hanky-panky.

Iranian teenagers were masters of covert tasks. The Persian expression of "she talks with her eyes" is true. We believe a woman's eyes are the strongest weapon she has against the opposite sex.

In the end, the teacher would totally surprise the rest of the students by marrying the girl. *This is how it works in the East.* Usually any girl of 18 years old or under marries the first and only man she meets.

To see Bijan once a week and sit beside him was my dream come through. The butterflies in my stomach were impossible to tame at the time of his arrival. At every accidental hand touch, I yearned. Like any Hollywood movie, he would grab and kiss me, *such a fantasy*.

In the library, we were always alone, but a thin wall divided us with Baba or Maman in the next room. The entire house was hushed so that we could even hear a drop of a needle. Bijan never tried to show any affection, not even holding my hand. I could not, however, deny my desire for him. Deep inside, I was quite certain he had special feelings for me, but he was too shy or too religious to show it.

At the last session, he whispered, "Mitra, with no doubt you'll be successful in your exam."

"Thank you," I beamed. "Any job prospective for you?"

He shrugged. "I've done some interviews. None is promising."

To keep our conversation going, I whispered. "What's the next move for you?"

He lowered his voice. "To go to America."

I met his piercing gaze when he continued, "I'd stay if I found a job with great pay."

At the door, I reached my hand to him. "I hope to see you again." Our handshake took much longer than usual.

My longing to see Bijan was mounting. As much as dating was not official, my generation created a covert life of our own.

Bahar, my buddy from high school, had to be the luckiest one. She was seeing a boy for almost three years and was in love with him without her parents having any idea. The minute she finished high school, her boyfriend sent his mother to ask for her hand in marriage. When Bahar stood up to her father's dissent and confessed her love for him, no one even questioned how she came to love him. So, her dad gave her permission to get engaged until he found a job. I missed her engagement party for I had to study; like the horse pulling a carriage and wearing blinders, I could only see the path of education for me.

Two weeks later, after two full-day exams, the announcement

of the passing students' names published in the daily newspaper. Baba did not wait for the daily delivery man. Instead, that early afternoon, he walked to the nearby stand and bought a copy.

When he returned home, I rushed to him, "Baba, did I?"

His somber face was my answer. I started crying and ran to my room. Our house turned into a funeral home. That night no words, or dinner for any one. A sea of sorrow drowned all of us.

Two months passed, then I applied for a scholarship to study in America. Meanwhile, Bijan and I saw each other once in a while. When I was going out, I told my parents that I was going to Bahar's house. Being dishonest with them ripped me up inside. I would pay any price to see Bijan.

Bahar repeated over and over, "Mitra, your parents are strange. They don't let you go with your friends across the street. But they let you go to a foreign country where boys and girls are together."

I held my silence.

One evening at dinner time, I opened the conversation, "Baba, I wonder. If I receive the scholarship to America, you'll let me go, without even knowing what I do over there. Why don't you let me go out with a *boyfriend* to see a movie or to a cafe?"

He washed down his mouthful of food and responded, "American society is different from ours."

Maman swallowed the rice and lamb, then voiced, "Dear, over there, boys and girls grow up together, so for their parents, dating is normal."

"Don't you trust me and my judgment?"

"Yes, I do," Baba replied. "But think. In the West, after eighteen, boys and girls are in charge of their own life. To make it or break is up to each individual."

Maman verbalized the truth of our society. "If a relative or a friend sees you with a boy in a cafe or theater, there would be gossip from here to eternity."

"Think of how you would be thought of then." Baba could not cover his sad voice.

As usual, our discussions did not satisfy me. *It is what it is. A vast gap between the Eastern and Western society.*

After passing several exams and interviews, I received a scholarship to study in America. Instead of being happy, I was still hopeful that Bijan would ask me to marry him. Then both of us could be together over there. I contacted him to meet for a cup of coffee. When we sat across from each other, I blurted out, "I got the scholarship to study in America!"

He beamed. "Congrats, very proud of you, Mitra."

"I'm thinking not to go."

His worried look was disturbing. "Why not?"

I put my elbows on the table and casually responded, "To marry, like other girls."

Bijan took a sip of his café glacé. "Your parents, especially your father, yearns for your grand achievements."

"If I were smart, I would've passed the university exam."

"Mitra, don't beat yourself up," He counseled. "Only ten percent of ten thousand applicants pass the exam."

"Yes, the competition is stiff." I tried to swallow the knot in my throat.

"They choose some of these applicants among *Savak* families, or they themselves are agents."

"What is Savak?"

Bijan lowered his voice. "A secret agency established by the Shah with the help of the CIA in 1957."

I hushed my voice as well. "Are these students spies?"

While drinking he acknowledged in agreement.

"What are your plans?" I forced myself to ask him the ultimate question, "Are you thinking of having a family soon?"

"Not really, I'm still trying to see if I'm able to go to America." He gazed into my eyes.

A few months later, without seeing or saying 'goodbye' to him, with a heavy heart, I flew out of Iran toward a bright future, as everyone believed.

Bahar said loudly at the airport, "Say hello to the handsome Sidney Poitier from Iranian girls!"

"Will do!" I responded laughing. "I'm sure, he'll be at the airport when I arrive!"

"Of course," Bahar hugged me. "He knows, you represent all Iranian girls, and he comes to welcome you." I kissed her, swallowed the knot in my throat, and stepped toward an unknown future.

13

1972

DURING THE FIRST few months of my studying at UCLA, Bahar and I communicated via letters. I learned that Bijan also left Iran. Thanks to Bahar's detective work, she sent me his number. To hear his voice on the phone was pure bliss.

"Mitra, it's good to hear from you." His friendly voice was void of passion and excitement.

I tried to muffle my loud thumping heart. "The same here, where are you?"

"I'm in Vancouver, British Columbia."

"How come? Not in America?"

"It didn't work out." He sounded disappointed. "You're in America, aren't you?"

" In L.A. and studying hard," Without giving him a chance to answer, I blurted out, "are you married now?"

"No. The Canadian girls aren't as pretty as Iranian girls." He uttered.

During the next few months, our repeat phone calls had never escalated to a higher level of intimacy. It seemed like I was talking with a girlfriend, but absent of any giggles—dry and formal. I was too reserved to have a talk with him heart to heart. In one of our conversations, he suggested, "How would you like to visit Vancouver? It's a beautiful city."

"I'd love that." After hanging up, I thought. He said no words of love or any other words of endearment to me.

When spring break rolled in, I packed my bag and journeyed to Vancouver. The beauties of city bedazzled me. In my inexpensive room at a budget motel, the window opened to a range of mountains against the sharp blue water. The mainland, attached to North Lonsdale Shore, put me in awe. The vacated site of North Van Ship Repair, a major shipyard during World War II, was, however, a sore thumb to the entire natural beauty of the city.

Bijan never took me to his place. According to him, he had rented a room from a family in the area, close to my hotel. Being a chemist, he worked odd hours. We saw each other once a day, whether for breakfast or dinner. I had to be alone during my three-day, four-night trip. The ferry from my hotel to downtown enabled me to tour Gastown, Chinatown, and Granville Island. The buses full of passengers, mostly couples, made me feel as if a bottomless pit had swallowed me. To pull me out, I grasped to its glamor.

On the last night, as soon as both of us sat down at a fish and chips place, I got right to it: "Bijan, we never talked about our future."

"I'm starving," he said nonchalantly and reached to cut the loaf of bread.

"Or our relationship." No way to deny my inside bewilderment.

He took a bite of bread. "Are you telling me when you leave we won't be friends anymore?" His eyes searched for a reply in mine.

"For how long?" I said, while looking up at the ceiling to prevent my tears from falling.

As long as we live." His giggle was jarring.

I kept quiet.

"I would love to be friends with you." His voice became serious. "You, unlike other girls, never bring up the subject of marriage." He looked straight into my eyes again. "You have your independent life, and I have mine."

"Is there any hope for us?" I implored. "One day to be more than friends?"

His face turned red as if it was on fire. He shook his head.

I pressed the issue. "Why not?"

"I'm sorry. I haven't been quite honest with you." To avoid my eyes, he turned his head and looked around the restaurant.

I pretended I hadn't noticed he was ignoring me. "If we're friends, there shouldn't be any secret between us."

"Correct." He looked down and, after a moment, raised his head. "For intimacy, I like men."

I could not believe my ears. I was dumbfounded.

"You shouldn't be angry with me," he rushed to say. "You've acted as if you like girls more than boys, too. You've never pushed or talked with me about marriage." He sounded annoyed.

Through my teeth, I claimed, "I'm not angry at you." His anguished eyes were hard to ignore. "By seeing you in secret, I've shown my passionate love for you." I wiped away my tears.

"I'm neither a mind reader nor a heart reader." He sighed. "Especially in our society, no girl becomes a friend with a boy just for the sake of friendship, except you."

Even in my culture, I'm the ugly duckling.

Back at UCLA, Like a robot that could not function, I drowned myself in the world of illusion to forget Bijan and my misery.

Here, in America, to see a movie was not that exciting. For me to afford the price of a ticket, I had to see a matinee, and after leaving the theater, the daylight bothered my eyes. But in Iran, theaters open in the early evening. When we exit, the outside is still dark. So, we stay in the world of darkness for a long time.

I looked at the list of films. They were either westerns, science-fiction, or comedy. However, *One Is a Lonely Number,* a drama, suited my situation. That afternoon, to forget Bijan and for a break from thinking of him, I walked to the movie theater close to campus. The ticket seller looked at me with sad eyes when I said, "One for *One is a Lonely Number.*" *How can it be? One is the number of unity and a complete number, it's impossible to be lonely.*

The film showed how a housewife, Amy, has a tough time coping with life after her husband, James, a professor, leaves her unexpectedly. Out of blue, one morning, he grabs a suitcase, dumps in some of his clothes, and moves in with his mistress. Soon, he files for divorce. Like some women, Amy prefers to ignore her husband's infidelities. She lives in a bubble pretending her marriage is perfect. She insists that one day James will be back. However, when she realizes he won't be back, she starts to find herself and her own passion in her single life, not relying on him. In the end, she makes *One*, a Perfect Number.

For sure, we are the same whether Easterners or Westerners, with the same wishes and desires. I walked out of the movie theater pretty much satisfied. I became decisive to make *me* a perfect number.

14

1973

IN THE FOLLOWING weeks and months, I kept asking myself, "How could my story not have a happy ending?" My destiny was not the same as most Iranian women's to get married. *But my story is not finished yet.* My only solution was to seek solace in the library.

On a Sunday afternoon, when I went to do my research for my course on Emerson, the place was full. After looking around, a small round table with two chairs at the far side was a pleasant remedy. A guy with blond hair and a white Polo shirt was sitting on one of them. I approached him.

"May I have this seat?"

He raised his head from his book and responded with a smile, "Of course, please!" His sky-blue eyes captured my heart. I was a sucker for blond hair and blue eyes.

"Are you a student here?" He stared into my eyes.

"Yes!"

"Are you French?"

I shook my head. "No, Persian."

His Nordic face lit up like the sun. "You're dressed elegantly, not like the rest of us with a shirt and jeans."

His denim pants were clean and looked new, not like most of the other students, torn on the knees or thighs. I did not think my tailored, cotton dress with colorful paisley patterns and my high-heel sandals were dressy at all.

His face reddened. "Where is Persia?"

"Persia or Iran."

He nodded. "Yes, we hear a lot about the Shah of Iran."

"I'm sure. He is a faithful friend of America." I came very close to saying, *American Puppet of Pahlavi,* according to my father, but I swallowed my words.

"I'm John Davis. What's your name?"

"I'm Mitra Tehrani."

He reached out his hand and we shook. "Wow, you're the first and only person I know from the Eastern part of the world." He closed his book and continued staring at me. "Now I remember. Last year the Shah held a 2,500-year celebration of the Persian Empire."

I smiled. "Some Western magazines called it, 'the most extravagant party in the history of humankind'."

My voice was full of pride when an old librarian with her thick, bifocal glasses came over and shushed us, in an angry voice, then exclaimed, "Here is not the place for conversation. Please step outside if you wish to chat."

John closed his book and stowed it in his backpack. "Let's get out of here. I'd love to hear more about this exorbitant party."

We sat down on a bench under a shade tree and he said, "Tell me more. But first, why did the Shah want to have such a celebration?"

I replied with excitement. "To show the world the new face of the Iranian ancient empire, a modern and proud Iran. A nation of black pearls, not of Islamic mullahs."

"By black pearls, do you mean oil?" He reached and gently touched my hand.

I nodded.

"Sorry for the interruption. Go on."

"I don't know what you all would do if your president ever had such an extraordinary celebration?"

"Don't divert, Mitra. Take me to the dream world of the East."

"We, the people, never know the details. But, some Western reporters who were lucky to be there, called it, 'a magical party' like in *One Thousand and One Nights.*"

"Were you there, Mitra?"

"No, I was already here. If I were there, I would've received an invitation." A smile covered my face when I stared into his ocean-color eyes to see if he got my joke.

"Really?"

I burst out laughing.

"Okay, kidding aside, I'll be hushed." John pulled an imaginary zipper across his mouth.

"In 1970, a year prior to this marvelous party, a French architect and his crew were hired to design and build fifty tent-like suites for the heads of state between the ruins of Persepolis, the ancient capital of the Persian Empire, and King Cyrus' tomb. Each tent had two bedrooms, two baths, an office, and a lavishly furnished salon that could accommodate twelve people."

"Wow!" John exclaimed.

"It's hard to imagine, isn't it?" I took a breath.

John affirmed.

"The arrangement for the tents was along five avenues, radiating out from a fountain. The main tent, measuring 75 yards by 26 yards was to be the banquet hall. For building these tents, they used 23 miles of silk. One German reporter called this city, 'Billion-Dollar Camping.'"

"So astonishing!" John wiggled on the bench, and his baby blue eyes were getting bigger by the minute.

I continued, "They flew all the items for the party from Paris. They were almost 9,000 pounds of beef, pork, lamb, fowl, and game birds, along with 2,500 bottles of champagne, one thousand Bordeaux, and 1000 Burgundy, all packed in 410 crates, delivered to a cellar which was built especially for this purpose in Persepolis four weeks before the celebration. Even ice, parsley, and chives were Parisian."

"Are you saying," John could no longer keep quiet, "in your country, there are no ice or vegetables?"

"We do. But, apparently, they aren't good enough for the dignitaries."

John read lots of enthusiasm in my voice and stood up. "Do you mind, if we go to the cafeteria, have something to drink, and continue there?"

"Not at all." I had a dry throat and welcomed a break. "Good idea, let's go."

After we paid for our drinks and sat down, John said, "What else can you tell me about this far-fetched party?"

"Come to think of it, not *everything* came from Paris. The 67 pounds of Iranian Caviar, the most superb caviar in the world, was from the Caspian sea, in the north of Iran." I had a sip of my iced tea. "I forgot to mention. They planted an entire forest next to the Persepolis to create the cool weather of Paris. Then, they brought 50,000 exotic songbirds were flown in from Europe."

"How amazing!" It was impossible for him to hide his excitement.

"But, three days later they all died."

"Why?" His voice was somber.

"Well, they weren't used to the desert climate." I paused. "I don't understand why they didn't fill this man-made forest with nightingales?"

"Do you have a lot of them in Iran?"

I affirmed, "Iran is famous for being the 'Land of Roses and Nightingales.'"

"How hot does it get?"

"Persepolis is in the south of Iran. Even though the celebration was held in mid October, during the day it gets up to well over 104, and at night to freezing temperatures."

"Mitra, which city are you from?"

"Tehran. It's a two-hour flight to Shiraz, the closest city to Persepolis."

"Is the climate the same in Tehran as in Persepolis?"

"No, Tehran lays at the skirt of Mount Alborz way north of Iran. We get snow in the winter and hot days in the summer, but cool at nights."

John asked. "Why do you refer to your country sometimes as Iran, and sometimes as Persia? Was there a name change?"

"No, among its natives, it's always called Iran after our Aryan race."

"The same race as Germans," John confirmed.

In agreement, I went on, "A group of Caucasians from an Aryan subrace divided into two. One went to Europe and established today's Germany. Another went to Asia and called their land Iran after their race."

"Then, where did Persia come from?"

"When the Greek historian, Herodotus, wrote the history of the Eastern world, he called the land Persia, and its people Persians."

"Now, it makes sense." John moved his head in affirmation. "Tell me, how much did the party cost the taxpayers?"

"According to one report, the Shah spent between 300 million to two billion Swiss francs."

Wow! No wonder they called it an extravagant party."

"I bet the Shah didn't even blink when he spent his people's money."

"How could he?" John said. "Don't you have a law that your lawmakers must approve the spending of the Shah?"

I shook my head and replied, "The Shah responded to his critics. 'Should I serve heads of state bread and radishes?' He was referring to the poor Iranian laborers who have flatbread and radishes for their lunch."

"What does your father do?"

"He had a newspaper, but he closed it down when I was a little girl."

"How come?"

"He hoped to bring down the glittery tapestry with which the Shah had covered our eyes."

"And of course, he couldn't," John acknowledged.

With a nod I confirmed it.

"What does he do now?"

"He has a print shop. And my mother is a teacher."

By this time, it was getting quite dark. "What about you, John? Tell me what are you studying?"

He was in his last year of law school and upon his completion, he'd go back to his hometown, Chicago. After we exchanged phone numbers, he said. "I'll call you sometime. Do you like to dance?"

"I love to."

"Disco?"

"I don't know what it is. I can only dance the Twist."

"It's not as hard as you may think; just move your body." He performed a smooth dance move that made me smile. *He's interested in my culture, and funny too. So amazing!*

A few days later, I heard from John. He indeed invited me to go dancing and arrived to pick me up at 8 o'clock on the following Friday night.

As soon as we entered Vigil Hollywood, I felt all of the difficulties of my studying in a foreign land melt away. I loved the happy beat of the music and dismissed the musty smell mixed with thick cigarette smoke permeating the cavernous room. The large glass sphere that hung from the ceiling was turning and filtering through the dusk with a delicate rainbow. The lights were all dimmed as if they were taking an inferior position to the Disco Ball. There were a few empty round tables arranged with chairs positioned two-thirds of the way to the raised stage where most of the people were congregating around. I was mesmerized. When John touched my shoulder, I felt as if I was in a dreamworld. He asked. "What would you like to drink?"

"I don't know, maybe water?"

He raised another question, "Have you had any alcohol drinks, like beer or wine before?"

I shook my head. "When I was ten or eleven, one time at dinner time my father was drinking beer, I was curious to know its taste. He offered me some and after a sip, I got sick." I made a sour face. "That was the end of my drinking."

"Would you like to try something?"

"You choose."

"How about a Shirley Temple?"

I was unable to make any sense of his silly smile.

After I tasted it, he said, "I doubt you'll get sick on this. How do you like it?"

I was not very much a fan of its sweet aftertaste, but, being polite, I said, "It's okay."

John gave a big smile from ear to ear. "Mitra, it doesn't have any alcohol in it."

"Oh, you're pulling my leg. Thanks."

Both of us laughed. To makeup, he got me a glass of white wine.

I loved it when we went to the stage. He was patient in teaching me how to disco.

It was around 11 when we pulled up to my dormitory. I started getting out and opened my mouth to thank him.

"Mitra wait. I'll walk you to the door."

"It's not that far."

"I know, but," he paused. "Did you have a good time?"

"Oh, yes, and I learned a lot. Disco dancing, and the difference between wine and a Shirley Temple. Thank you so much."

He held on tight to the steering wheel, "I wish I was free to date you."

I hid my disappointment and in a cheery voice I teased, "Was my dancing that bad?"

His upper lip winced. "No, it's not that. We can hang out once in a while, as friends, but it can't get serious."

"And that would be fine," I replied evenly. "As an Iranian girl, I don't give myself permission to get involved with an American. I have a scholarship, obligating me to return to Iran."

"If I were free, I wouldn't mind going to Iran with you."

My heartbeat escalated. "What do you mean?"

"See, I have a fiancé in Chicago. We'll wed once I finish law school."

"It works for the best," I said steadfastly, though my heart wasn't. "I'm not able to be more than just a friend either."

John pushed his hair away from his broad forehead and looked at me shockingly. "Are you telling me that boys and girls in Iran do not date?"

"That's what I'm saying." Then Bahar's face came to me. "If we do, it's in secret."

"Wow! Then, how do you all know you're in love and want to marry?"

"We don't. Most Iranians' marriage is a leap of faith, for it's an arrangement of the parents. There is no other choice for 'good' boys and girls."

"Was your parents' marriage arranged?"

"No, actually my parents fell in love. They were distant family members and met at a social gathering."

"Hmm!" He got out of the car.

I hopped out too.

He came around the car and said, "As a gentleman, I wanted to open the door for you. Don't Iranian men open the car door for women?"

"I *can* open the door. Why do I need a man to open it for me?"

"I guess you all do things differently over there."

My answer to him was only a half-hearted nod.

It would be very difficult to live in another culture, especially if one wants to be part of the melting pot. A grown-up, like a baby, must learn everything from scratch, I thought when I closed my eyes.

After about six months, a student from the next dormitory invited me to a Mary Kay Cosmetics' facial party. All four of us sat in the dining room of the hostess who was representing the company. After the facial, I loved the products and the way they worked. It was perfect for some Iranian housewives, or girls without many years of education. I signed up to be a representative. Then, could get the rights of importing it to Iran and train some Iranian girls to sell the product. *Almost all of us, rich or poor, love to use cosmetics.*

To give parties, I had to drive all over Los Angeles, and public transportation was not reliable. In addition, I had to carry a huge display case and two other bags with me each time I gave a private party. To buy a car, the campus paper ads were my best bet. After some searches, a 1960 Volkswagen known as the Beetle was all I could afford. It was invented in Germany in 1937, during Hitler's era, with its engine in the rear as opposed to other cars. Baba Nima had one for quite a while. This purchase was a reminder of Baba each time I used it.

One day, Judy, one of my classmates in the Faulkner class, wanted me to give a party on the upcoming Saturday to her mother and some of their friends. They lived in Santa Barbara, about a three-hour drive from UCLA. When I looked at my calendar, it was the same Saturday that I had a date with John in Vigil Hollywood. But it was not until at 7:30 PM. After some calculations, I scheduled the party for 10:00 AM. *I'll have plenty of time. I should be back no later than five.*

On that Saturday, my party was a success, and I sold some skincare creams, mascara, and lipsticks, but not much to make a dent in my bags. Judy and her mother insisted I stayed for lunch. I left their house around 3:00 PM. After driving for about forty-five minutes, I heard. *BOOM! BOOM!* The sound of the car scared me.

I had taken the scenic Pacific Highway, a two-way road, instead of the freeway. I slowed down and tried to turn the steering wheel toward the right. My Beetle groaned and whined as if it just woke up from a deep slumber. On the road-shoulder, the engine stopped. I tried and tried to start it. *Rur, rur, rur* was the only response. I found myself in a dire situation. It wouldn't be prudent to get out to hitch a ride home, not in my fancy dress suitable for disco dancing, and high heel shoes with perfect makeup. Also, in my culture, it's a no-no to take a ride from a stranger. I stayed put and wait for a police car to arrive.

After fifteen minutes or later, among several cars zooming by and rattling my car, a truck pulled and stopped in front of me. A man dressed in cowboy gear came to the window.

"Lady, what's the problem?"

I was reluctant to talk with a stranger but hopeful that he might help. I responded, "No idea."

"Mind if I look?"

"Thank you. Please go ahead."

When he approached the front of the car, I lost all my confidence in him. He opened the hood, and screamed, "I don't know how to fix a car with a pink case instead of an engine. Then slamming the hood, shook me when I saw he climbed back into his truck. After blowing the horn, a gravel or two hit my windshield.

I waited, waited, and waited some more. The sun set early, being the end of November. I could not even see the citrus trees or fields of strawberries. Whenever I pictured John walking up and down outside the Virgil Hollywood entrance door, my stomach turned. He'll be angry and think I stood him up.

At last, a car pulled to a stop behind me. Into the rearview mirror, I saw a middle-aged man with a girl around 10 get out of a new station wagon. He approached me from the passenger's side. I reached over and rolled down the window a little with a shaky hand.

He said, "Ma'am, I'm Paul, and this is my daughter, Silvia. I'm a mechanic. Do you mind if I look at the engine?"

"Please do."

With a flashlight, he looked and touched some parts of the engine for a few minutes. Then he closed the hood and came to me with his daughter tagging along. "Ma'am, your car needs a major repair. Are you going to Los Angeles?"

"Yes, I'm a student at UCLA."

"Silvia and I live in Santa Monica. If you would like, we can give you a ride. Westwood is not very far out of our way."

It was already way past nine, and fear overcame me. I trusted this father and climbed into the back seat. Throughout the ride, in my heart, I could not wait to get to my dorm and call John to apologize for not showing up at Virgil Hollywood. When we arrived in front of my dorm, I saw John's car.

"Gosh! This is my friend's car," I gasped.

I got out, and John approached me with worry etched on his face. "Mitra, are you alright?"

I nodded and introduced John to Paul and Silvia; then he briefed John on my predicament.

I offered to pay Paul for his generosity, but he wouldn't take my money. After they left, I was expecting John would be upset. I asked, "How come you're here?"

"It concerned me when you didn't show. You're not like that to just blow off a friend."

"So very kind of you," I uttered.

John said, "It's not safe for your car to be on the road. Let's go to my place. I'll call a friend who has a truck and a heavy-duty towing chain."

"Now? Let's wait until Monday morning."

"Yes. Now. Your car may not be there by Monday." He led me to his car and opened the door for me.

At his apartment, he, the good-natured guy that he was, asked, "Have you had anything to eat?"

I was famished and shook my head.

After making a sandwich, he called his friend. The three of us then went and towed my car that night and left it by the repair shop for Monday.

When John dropped me at my dorm, I thanked him from the bottom of my heart; then said, "John, it doesn't matter where each one of us ends up to be. I want you to know that you have the highest place in my heart forever."

A few months later, John received his law degree and left UCLA. I heard no more from him. To know a Western man who looks after another ones' interests instead of only his, gave me hope that one day, I could find a partner like him. He did not betray his fiancé and he helped me, just like helping another human being. *All of that leaves a delicious taste in my mouth.*

15

1983

MONDAY MORNING did not come soon enough for me in Boston. After reading the letters in Farsi signed by Majid, I understood he had a vast network for locating the Iranians disloyal to the Khomeini regime. But there was nothing incriminating, or that would hold up in a court of law. Then, I came up with a plan and ready to take my chances.

I went to Georgina after locating a Persian restaurant close to his house. "What are you doing for lunch?"

She shrugged. Her somber look with dark circles around her eyes was in contrast to her cheerful face of the last Friday. She mumbled. "No idea, dear."

In my enthusiastic voice, I asked. "How does Persian food sound?"

"Sounds great." She licked her lips, looked up, and said. "I love the fluffy rice with saffron."

"It's my treat."

"Even more delicious." She grinned and continued, "Let me finish this report. I'll come and get you."

A cab dropped us off in front of the Shahrzad Restaurant. Inside, I combed through the crowd. There was no sign of Majid. Then, I pointed to an unoccupied table near the entrance door, and requested the hostess, "Is this table available?" Anyone walking in could not miss it. I sat on the chair facing the door.

Georgina and I started looking at the menu.

"This can't be, Mitra! Is that you?"

I raised my head upon hearing my name, squinted my eyes, and looked for a moment at his face. Then I broke into a bemused smile and said, "Hey Majid? What a surprise! What are you doing here?" I smiled slyly and without giving him a chance to respond, I said, "Are you following me again?"

We both had a friendly laugh. Without waiting, he reached his hand to Georgina and said, "I'm Majid. Mitra and I've known each other for a long time." He then turned to me, "Lady Mitra, so nice to see you again. I thought you were in L.A."

"How are Negar and Nasim?"

"They're good."

"Do you live in Boston now?"

Majid nodded.

"Great! I would love to see dear Negar."

"They're gone to Shiraz."

I turned to Georgina and said, "The beautiful city near the ruins of Persepolis."

"Listen, Lady Mitra," Majid responded, "once in a while, I get together with some Persian friends to discuss world events. Would you like to join us sometime?"

"I would love that." I looked for one of my business cards in my purse when Gorgina asked, "Majid, would you like to join us?"

"No, thanks." He gave her a warm smile. "I'm meeting some friends." He pointed to another side of the room and raised his hand to them. After taking my card and looking at it, he said, "I'll call you." He paused a moment and looked at me. "I leave you ladies to have your lunch in peace." He proceeded to his friends' table.

Georgina picked up the menu and with a smile said, "How do you know this handsome guy?"

I turned a deaf ear to her. "Let's order. I'm starving." To pull off the ruse delighted me.

Upon my return to the office, a secretary had taken a message and placed it on my desk. It was from Robert. *He remembered!*

I called him back that evening. Unable to see each other during the week, we agreed to have brunch on the upcoming Saturday.

During the week, I pored over the letters in Farsi and translated them into English. None of them showed any smoking gun pointing to Majid's guilt. He could be innocent or masterful at his covert task. Perhaps he was just a middle man, and the mastermind of the operation was someone else. *Hossain, in Zurich, perhaps? Or Hojat, or someone else whose name doesn't mention in any of these letters.* It was also possible that these letters are written in codes that only his group understand it. I kept wondering.

When I returned the translated letters, the bureau also could not confirm Majid's guilt. They instructed me to wait for his phone call. Then to meet him and his friends, I had to wear a wire.

After two weeks, Majid called and invited me to the gathering at his house. "Mitra this coming Friday night, can you make it?"

I agreed with no hesitation. Even though I already knew where he lived, I asked. "What's is your address?"

After I hung up the phone, it occurred to me: *Gosh*, Friday. I had a special date with Robert. At last, he was successful in getting a reservation at the Union Oyster House restaurant at the booth dedicated to President Kennedy on the *same* Friday night. "Dear Mitra," I recalled Robert's words, "it'll be so exciting to sit in the same seat where President Kennedy sat."

But, I had to disappoint him and cancel it. Robert and I were going steady. His kind way of treating me had me head over heels in love with him. Each time I looked into his intense eyes, my heart melted. Likewise, he acted as if he'd found his life purpose, to please me. Several times he said, "Darling Mitra, you're the light of my life."

Feeling in love and had never touched by love like this before.

This evening, at the end of work, I rushed to the beautiful restaurant, Reel House, at the harbor to meet him. As a civil engineer, he went out of town on and off. He was back in town after being away for a week. My anxiety, however, did not leave me alone on how to break the news to him.

As soon as our eyes met, his handsome face lit up. We hugged. Like a gentleman, he helped me with my overcoat. His gentle yet strong touch put him one step closer to winning my heart. After our drinks, the host led us to the dining room. I tried to calm my nerves by looking out of the huge windows and concentrating on the high waves slamming the seashore. We sat side by side and Robert put his hand on my knee. "I'm madly in love with you, Mitra."

I could not respond. *See how madly you're in love when you hear I can't make it.*

When the waiter set our grilled Salmon in front of us,

Robert, in his jolly voice whispered, "Dear, we're all set for Friday night at 7:00. I'll pick you up at 6:30."

Without looking at him, I murmured, "So sorry, dear, something related to work came up. You understand, don't you?" I squeezed his hand.

When I raised my head, his face was not joyful anymore. He put his wine glass down and surprised me by responding in anger, "What could it be more important than having dinner at Kennedy's booth?"

"Dear, I'm very disappointed too. It's a meeting I can't get out of."

His suspicion was clear in his voice, "Who has a meeting on a Friday night?"

Agent Wilson's words reverberated in my head. *You must swear to the secrecy of this assignment. Never, ever divulge it to anyone, not even your sister.*

I sighed and breathed my words, "Dear, my notorious boss calls impromptu staff meetings. No excuse is acceptable to him unless we are dead, or eager to be fired. And if I lose my job, I won't be able to stay in Boston. Don't you know a translating job is impossible to come by?"

Robert picked up the fork and started piercing the fish repeatedly while grumbling, "Tonight, the fish is no good."

We ate our dinner in silence. When we came out, Robert rushed to excuse himself, claiming to be tired. I noticed this was not the first time he acted like a brat when he didn't get his way. I understood we all have two sides to us. But, it seemed like he couldn't handle very well the two-year-old still living inside of him.

Throughout the week, my thoughts were clumsy and confused. They streaked and broke up like pictures on a flickering television screen. My mind traveled to Ben and Rome when I dialed the number to inform the Agency about the day and time of the gathering in Majid's house.

On Friday, at 6:00, two women came to my place and wired me up. At seven, I rang the bell of the Harbor Towers with a trembling hand. To calm down my breathing I repeated: *This is the most important task in my life and I must do it for Ben's sake.*

I stepped out of the elevator on the twelfth floor and saw Majid was waiting by his apartment's door. The chandeliers, Persian rugs, and the furniture were more regal than his place in Zurich. He led me to a room with a bloodwood table, twelve matching chairs, and a long credenza against an enormous wall. The silk Persian rug that covered the floor had to be a special order.

I looked at the empty chairs. "I must be the first one here." *Or maybe he is lying like in Zurich.*

He smiled. "Have you forgotten our culture?"

I knew well what he was getting at. "If the invitation is for seven..." he completed my sentence, "we are lucky if the guests show up at nine."

We both laughed, and I asked, "How are Nasim and Negar?"

"Good, I talked with Negar this morning. She goes to school now."

"Doesn't Nasim want to come here?"

He shook his head, then walked to the kitchen to get some fresh-brewed tea. The walls grabbed my attention. The etched names of Allah, Mohammad, and Ali in gold or silver-framed, made out of mosaic inlaid wood and ivory, called khatam covered the walls. There was no doubt in my mind that I had entered a hard-core Moslem's house.

Soon, a young lad, Ahmad, arrived. His skin was darker than mine. He had to be from the south of Iran, by the Persian Gulf. A little later, Hojat, who looked to be about 60, with white hair and a heavy beard, showed up. For the first time, being the only woman among three men and not knowing them well made me uneasy. I swallowed my cough, knowing that my "shadow" was listening. In addition, if any of these men jeopardized my safety, I could use the secret word and help would arrive. But for Ben's sake, I do my best not to endanger the assignment.

Majid, as a devout Moslem, started, "*Besme-Allah*, in the name of Allah, the hand of Allah sent our Imam Khomeini…"

"Long live Imam Khomeini!" The other men raised their voices, and I echoed their chant.

Majid continued. "To rescue us from the corrupt Shah."

"Lady Mitra," Ahmad started while his eyes fixed on the floor, adhering to the Islamic law not to stare into my face, "it's refreshing to see a lady interested in what proud men have to say."

"I'm ready to listen to any words or do anything to bring down the enemies of our Supreme Leader, and Islam."

I looked at everyone and sipped my tea.

Hojat interjected in a spiteful voice. "Let's talk about the way we are eager to cleanse our society."

Majid finished in his low voice, "And make sure Iranians, especially our youths are free from the sinful life that the nefarious Shah had promoted."

I nodded. "You are right, Majid. The Shah only showed us the road of corruption and nothing else." Then, I took yet another sip of Darjeeling tea, its sweet scent calmed my nerves.

"Lady Mitra," Hojat turned to me. Unlike Ahmad, he held

his head up high and asked in an accusatory tone, "Why are you here? Why don't you go back to Iran?"

I wondered if he was the leader of the group.

Before I could make up an excuse, Majid rushed in like a referee. "Hojat Khan, I've known Lady Mitra for a long time. No need to question her."

To offer something credible, I responded, "Allah's will," and hid the storm inside me with a smile.

Then Majid came closer to the table, looked at me with his gunmetal eyes. "Let's talk about our plan and familiarize Lady Mitra. I'm sure after she hears our holy mission, she agrees to join us."

"I'm lost." I shifted in my chair and asked, "To join what?"

Ahmad muttered like a fire under ashes, "Our team to preserve the Islamic Republic of Iran."

"Oh," matter-of-factly I said, "nothing is more important than watering the seed of our holy regime and see it becomes a sturdy tree." I had to wrestle with my cough to keep it down. Ignoring the jabbing of the wire, I became focused on listening to Majid saying, "Or anyone with a connection to the tyrant Shah."

"Lady Mitra," Hojat grumbled. "Now do you get what we do?"

I nodded and raised my empty cup to Majid. He went and brought the teapot to the table, then poured some in my cup. I held my hands around it. Its warmth soothed my soul. "Please, continue. I'm all ears now."

The three men talked for over an hour. All about how wonderful the new regime was to divide the responsibilities in Iranian society between men and women, the way our Prophet intended. I wanted to get up and scream at them, *You ignorant men! You must understand what Mohammad instructed us.* Instead, I maintained a face eager to hear more.

Once in a while, I chimed in, "Allah is great!" or "*Marg*, death, to the supporters of the Shah!"

One time I shouted, "Mr. Hojat, you're right! We need to bring the traitors of the Islamic Republic of Iran to justice."

When Majid finished the meeting with *Allah-o'-Akbar*, Allah is great. I got up to leave. But he signaled me to sit back down. After the other two left, he asked, "Mitra, what do you think?"

"You have a saintly task before you, and I admire you for it." I hoped my subterfuge had been successful and had won over his approval.

He began nodding his head. "Lady Mitra, I'm very impressed. I didn't know you are so much in favor of our holy regime."

"Thank you, Majid Khan. I had no occasion before to reveal my true beliefs."

"It'll be great if you become part of our group and help us go after the betrayers. Would you like that?"

I blinked my eyes as if taken by surprise. "Yes! Thank you for considering me worthy to be in your group."

"Excellent!" he replied, "Then let's get started." Majid reached into a pocket of his jacket and produced a picture of a woman in Islamic hijab. "Don't let this woman, Donya, fool you with a scarf covering her hair. She attends prayers at the mosque every Friday eve. Go there and establish a friendship with her. Find out where she places her loyalties."

I nodded, took the picture, and left his apartment. I decided more than ever to bring down the tapestry hiding Ben's death. As yet I had no evidence Majid did it. *Was it Majid? Maybe. Was it Ahmad? Not likely, he seems too young. Was it Hojat? It could be. He seems even more radical than Majid. Could it be Hossain in Zurich? It can't be this woman, Donya, or Majid would invite her tonight.*

The following Thursday, after dinner, I wore a scarf and set out to the mosque. As a teenager, I had gone to the neighborhood mosque once or twice with my friends in Tehran. My parents, unlike Bahar's, were never eager to go to the mosque. One time I asked, "Baba, why do we never attend the mosque every Friday eve like some others?"

He looked at me askance. "By listening to a mullah, no one learns anything new. Besides, I'm opposed to the structured religion which most people blindly follow; especially since our politicians and clergymen have subverted its rules according to their whims."

At the entrance door to the mosque, I took off my shoes and placed them in one of the many pigeonholes. There were a few women sitting in the first row behind a curtain, separating them from men. Right away, I spotted Donya. There was a little girl, about eight or nine, sitting next to her. The seat by the child was empty. I went over and sat beside her. She turned to me with a smile.

I murmured in Farsi, "What is your name, dear?"

The girl pulled the scarf closer to her forehead, turned to Donya, and shook her knee, "Mom!"

Donya turned to me. Her jet-black eyes were full of sorrow. "Hi, I'm Mitra."

In a kind voice, she answered, "I'm Donya and this is my daughter Suri."

At that moment, the mullah with his white turban and black cloak entered. Every one hushed until the break.

When the mosque attendant served hot tea in tumbler glasses

without saucers, I took a chance and started a conversation, "Are you new here, Lady Donya?"

"No, my family and I have been here for some time."

"I was born in Iran, though," Suri announced.

"Where in Iran, dear?"

Her mother replied, "In Shiraz."

Suri jumped in, "The city near Persepolis."

Then Donya uttered, "How long have you been here?"

"I'm a newcomer."

That night, Donya invited me to lunch at her house on the following Sunday. Right away, I contacted my invisible agent to ask about her. Within a day, I learned she was not in Majid's group, and they encouraged me to start a friendship with her for she might know more about him and his cohorts.

Juggling my work, dating, and the covert assignment left me fatigued. My only delight was Robert. He kept his sense of humor regardless of not being able to see me as often as he desired. He said over and over, "Darling Mitra, you work long hours. If I didn't trust you, I'd think you're dating a bunch of other men."

"Robert," I exclaimed, "By now, you should know. I don't date just for the sake of dating."

He scratched his head. "You've become like a fish. Each time I catch you, you slide right out of my hands."

We both burst out laughing.

∾16∾

1984

TO DISCOVER whether Majid was the one who caused Ben's death was my primary goal. Based on the information from the Agency about Donya, and my gut feelings, I tightened my friendship with her. We understood each other on a higher level. Our conversations came from our hearts.

One night during a visit, Donya started, "Mitra, I hope by now you've realized that Majid is a corrupt man, and has no fiber of humanity in him."

My eyes went wide and I asked, "How do you know?"

"Nasim and I were good friends during our school years." Donya paused. "When she married Majid, and I married Reza, our friendships became even stronger."

"So interesting."

She nodded and continued, "Not long after her marriage to Majid, Nasim disclosed to me how he battered her into submission."

"No wonder," I remembered, "whenever I saw her in Zurich, she always wore long sleeves." I put a sugar cube in my mouth and had a sip of my black tea. "To my understanding, she wanted Negar to have an Iranian education, and not to forget her Farsi."

"Well, it looks that way, doesn't it?" Donya said through her teeth. "That's not how it went down. Nasim wanted to come to America with him. But Majid sent her away."

"Why?"

"He wanted to get rid of her," Donya replied. "He played a trick on her."

"How so?"

"He desired to be a free man in the West, where no one looks into his business. And he could play around too." Donya swallowed hard. "He encouraged Nasim to return to Iran with Negar for a family visit. After a few months, she requested Majid, as her husband for a permission note to get her exit visa. Guess what he responded?"

"I'm afraid to," I said.

"He told her not to wait for any permission." Donya took a deep breath. "Stay there until her hair becomes the same color as her teeth."

I sighed. "As if darkness has covered his heart."

"Yes, or maybe even worse."

I gave some space to her silence.

"If it weren't for him," Donya went on, "my husband, Reza, God bless his soul, could be alive today." She started crying.

"So sorry," my words mixed with genuine sorrow. I couldn't believe what I heard next.

"In Iran, Majid joined Reza's group after the revolution." She pulled out a white handkerchief from her pocket. Its smell of rose water filled the room. After drying her wet eyes, she went on, "My husband believed the new regime is a radical movement, in opposition to what our Prophet Mohammad instructed." She took a deep sigh. "Two years ago while he was walking home," she paused and after a moment continued, "One of Majid's followers shot Reza in the back." She pointed to the sidewalk through the window. "Right there! He came so close to me, but yet so far." Her wailing ensued.

"How do you know it was one of Majid's followers?"

"Reza was receiving several threatening letters and phone calls that wanted him to renounce his allegiance to Khomeini." Donya breathed her words out. "Reza never took any of them seriously. He believed in America and that the Khomeini group could not bring him harm."

I hit my face and hugged her while both of us cried hard and loud. Then I asked her, "Dear, how come you couldn't prove his guilt?"

Donya sighed and through her tears said, "How could I? The perpetrator got away. No way to pin it on Majid. He was in Zurich."

At last, I revealed my deep-down secret, "Have you heard of Behnam?"

As if she received a shot of new blood, she exclaimed, "Ben Amirian, a senior diplomat, worked at the Iranian Embassy in Rome?"

I nodded.

After the sniffling, she said with disgust, "I have no proof, but I believe Majid did it. Because of his connection to the Khomeini group, he knew Ben was up for a promotion to become the ambassador. So, he fabricated a bunch of lies against him that he was loyal and had some connections with the Shah."

Wow! Here is another person in tears because of Majid. But I need solid proof to take him down.

"Dear Donya, did you report your husband's murder to the police?"

"Yes, I did. But the culprit had disappeared by then." She dried her tears. "And over time, Reza's file got lost among tons of other cold-cases."

"Why didn't you confront Majid?"

"My dear Mitra," Donya wailed, "my hands're tied. With a little girl to look after, I'm afraid Majid might do the same to Suri and me too."

"I understand."

When I left Donya's home, I was decisive to brew a way to cleanse the world of this diabolical creature, Majid.

At the Union Oyster House Restaurant, the server put down the birthday cake before me, and a few other ones sang, "Happy Birthday". Then Robert whispered to him, "We're ready for the champagne too."

The waiter snapped his fingers, and another one approached with the tulip-shape glasses. We picked up our glasses to toast when my eyes become bigger. At the bottom of my glass, there was a ring. I looked up to Robert and blushed. "What is this?"

He smiled. "See for yourself."

"Oh, my!"

"Mitra, I love you so much. Will you marry me?" He said from the other side of the table without kneeling.

"Yes," I took a deep breath, looked directly into his eyes, and felt at ease. "I love you more."

"Then, we need to talk about the date to tie the knot." He took a sip.

I remembered Agent Wilson's words: *No one, not even your sister is to be privy to your assignment.* I paused. When his anxious stare did not leave me, I breathed out, "Dear, we're not in a rush, are we?"

"Take your time. As long as you need." He flinched. "No doubt in *my* mind."

"Dear," I covered the raging storm within, and in a cheerful voice said, "you have my devotion. I'm committed to you. Let's have fun now and enjoy the present."

"I'll wait as long as it takes." He sealed our engagement with a kiss.

To be an undercover agent was taking a heavy toll on me. I felt I was drowning and unable to breathe. My coughing had escalated over the last few months. I was running out of time without completing my covert assignment.

Robert was pressing me to marry him. However, I couldn't take a leap of faith and endure a new role in my life. As long as we were in love and trusted each other, I did not see any need for a piece of paper to validate the constitution of our relationship.

To uncover Majid's deviousness torched my mind to no end. Over the next few weeks, I gained Majid's confidence by calling him twice a week expressing my distaste for the Shah, and my love for Khomeini and his regime. In addition, I sought the guidance from him on how to approach Donya and what questions to ask.

He became flattered and responsive. "You start by bad-mouthing our Imam Khomeini, and see her reaction."

"But," I just could not control my words, "isn't that being dishonest?"

"Mitra, don't think so deeply. You are on the Path of Divine, a little dishonesty won't hurt."

A little later on, after getting together with Donya, I called to report back to him. "Majid, you're right. She is a good actor *pretending* to love Khomeini."

"Great, Mitra! You've become a useful member of my team. Keep up the good work."

"Thank you. It's only a matter of time, and through Donya, I hope to learn the names of at least three or four other imposters to our holy regime."

And as I always finished my conversation, "Majid Khan, thank you for being my leader."

One day, I listened to a voice mail on my home answering machine: Your contact has a trip planned. He had purchased a one-way ticket, and in a couple of days, he is leaving for Iran, Canada? Or back to Switzerland?

If Majid bought a one-way ticket, very likely he would not be planning to return. *Is it possible he suspects me? There should still be* a window of opportunity to get the goods on him. It was difficult to play a hand which I despised some words that break my heart while acting calm and collected.

I left an urgent message with Majid informing him that the important information about Donya has resurfaced, and he needs to meet me in person. A cafe near his home was to be our place of rendezvous.

Even though I wasn't sure whether he'd show up, I got wired up. To my surprise, he walked in half an hour late. After shaking hands, he sat down. With an undertone of anger, he asked, "Mitra, what is so urgent? What did you learn from Donya?"

"I'll tell you in a minute, but first there's something I have to get off my chest."

Majid nodded to show *go ahead*.

I swallowed hard and put on my acting hat. "Majid, no way for me to believe I fell for such a traitor as Ben." I wiped my forehead. "To know how cleverly he duped me, and how his death crushed me, makes me feel like a fool. If only I'd known he was a double crosser," and then I said the cruelest words I'd ever spoken, "I would've felt joy instead. Ben got what he deserved."

Majid took a sip of his coffee. With a kind voice, he murmured, "Mitra, don't feel bad. In the end, justice was served."

I did my best to cover my trembling within when, in a decisive tone, I said, "Did you know Ben was a back-stabber while working with him as his assistant in Rome?"

In a grim voice, he responded, "What is your obsession with him? Is today Ben's day?" He snorted, "Now you're engaged, why do you care?"

I turned a deaf ear to his comment, mustered all my strength, and in a calm voice, I said, "I'm still learning and you are a *master*. How do you always remain so objective?"

That did it. As I'd hoped. I had just tapped his ego button. His mood changed. He began boasting like a hunter standing over his killed lion, beating his chest in triumph. "Everything I do is Allah's will. We are all merely pawns to do His bidding. I couldn't read what was truly in Ben's heart, but I felt Allah speaking to me: 'Do not take that risk!' So, I raised a red flag after learning that our holy regime was interested to elevate Ben to be the new ambassador."

I cut in, "Is that the reason the administrator summoned him to Tehran?"

"Kind of," Majid replied. "I orchestrated that by casting doubt upon his true allegiance. Ben was in contact with the last Shah's prime minister, Bakhtiar, in Paris."

I interrupted again for the sake of clarifying his statements. getting clarification "Wasn't Bakhtiar assassinated in Paris?"

"Yes." A wide smile covered his face from ear to ear. "Isn't it wonderful? That is also to my credit."

His voice jarred me. I had to hide the joy inside of me. But I had a moment of panic. *What if the wire didn't work?*

"So, you said you had information on Donya," Majid prompted me.

I looked left and right, then removed a sealed envelope from my purse and slid it across the table to him. "I think you'll be very interested to read this," and gave him a sly smile.

He started opening it.

"Not here," I cautioned him. "Read it when you get home."

He nodded and slipped the envelope into his jacket pocket. I had quite grown cautious by then. Inside the envelope was a blank sheet of paper. But as the saying goes, *Desperate times call for desperate measures.* I hoped he would never have time to see inside the envelope.

Majid signaled the waitress for the check.

"Please excuse me, before we go, I need to use the ladies' room."

In the restroom, I hurried over to the farthest stall and knocked three times. The door opened. There was my female CIA contact. She held up her hand while listening to someone in her earpiece and nodding. After a moment, she looked at me, gave a thumbs-up, and said. "We got it."

I breathed a big sigh of relief. Then, the CIA lady instructed me: "Leave the restaurant with him. As soon as you are outside, turn and go to your left."

When I exited the restroom, Majid had paid and was waiting. At the door, like a gentleman, he opened it for me, and we both exited.

Following her direction, as soon as I reached the sidewalk, I took several quick steps to my left, away from him. He turned and looked at me quizzically.

At the same moment, the doors of a black SUV, parked in

front of the restaurant, flew open. Three government men rushed toward Majid with guns drawn. He threw his hands in the air. The two CIA men cuffed him while the third one, in a clear voice, claimed, "Majid Enayati, you are under the arrest for conspiracy to commit murder." He then rattled off a list of other charges which my nervous mind could not make out.

Majid looked at me and was confused as he watched me undo the three top buttons of my blouse. I grabbed my collar, pulled it to one side, to reveal the wire. At the sight of wire, Majid became furious. "TRAITOR!"

I took a couple of steps toward him, peered into his eyes, and said, "This is for Ben!" Then I spat on his shoe.

Right away, CIA men took me in a separate car. During the debriefing, Agent Wilson impressed upon me that it would be in my best interests to keep mum and not to tell *anyone* about my CIA gig, including Robert.

To forget everything, especially Majid, I took the train to put as many miles between me and him. I sat on a bench at the Walden Pond and immersed my soul in the tranquility of this beautiful lake.

A few months later, I learned that Majid had squealed like a piglet hoping to lessen his sentence. He gave up the names of all his co-conspirators, Ahmad, Hojat, Hossain in Zurich, and several more. The CIA could shut down that part of the operation. They were more than pleased with me and what I had accomplished. They awarded me a handsome bonus and even allowed me to stay in Boston.

With the lump sum I received from the Agency, I could afford to buy a condo close to the harbor. They also helped me to find my dream job. Boston Hall Publishing House hired me as an assistant to the director. I couldn't be happier, to be surrounded by books, books, and more books.

Meanwhile, I melted under Robert's pressure, but instead of marrying him, I agreed to let him move in with me. Most of his engineering salary went to pay his debts from his previous marriage. I did not mind paying more than my fair share because I loved him. My father used to hammer in me: "Remember, Mitra. You are equal to a man. When both go out, if one time he pays the bill, you do the same next time."

To explain my windfall to Robert was that my paternal rich uncle back in Iran passed on. He had no survivors except my father. So, my parents sent the inheritance to me to fulfill an Iranian wish to buy rather than rent.

17

1986

LIFE WAS GOOD. And I was much happier drowning myself among books and manuscripts. I wish I could say the same about my relationship with Robert. Him pressuring me to marry bore no fruit. To leave my freedom on the altar was an impossible task. In my heart, I had a hard time convincing myself that our relationship would be stronger after the marriage. Sometimes, he challenged me with every decision I made. I could make no right choice. If I wore a white dress, it was tasteless. If it was colorful, he would question, "Have you forgotten you're pushing forty, and this dress is for a young girl?" He was a master at making me feel confused.

Every day, bright and early, Robert went to his construction firm and came home late at odd hours. During the days, he was too busy to even eat supper with me.

One night when we were eating together, I broke the silence, "After dinner, how about to sit on the porch and finish our wine?"

As if oblivious to my question, he resumed cutting his steak. The screeching knife hurt my ears. After a while, his head still bowed over his plate, he mumbled, "Why?"

"We spend little time together or don't talk like we used to."

He gobbled down his dinner, washed it off with the rest of his wine, and muttered, "Talk? Not tonight," then he went to bed.

I had heard the way to a man's heart is through his stomach. So the following night, I cooked his favorite dish, lasagna, from scratch and set the table decorating it with a fresh flower centerpiece and candles. By nine o'clock he was still a no show. I ate a few bites, which clogged my throat, fixed him a plate, and left it in the oven.

Upon his arrival, without saying a word as if I was invisible, he walked into the kitchen, took the plate out, emptied it into the garbage, and put it in the dishwasher. He stumbled to the bedroom.

His behavior created a load of confusion in me. Once, I was full of happiness, but not recently. I considered myself the saddest woman in the world. *I still love Robert the same way. But he changes like the weather, one day hot, one day cold.*

At last one evening, when my patience reached its boiling point, I asked, " Robert, are you having an affair?"

He flinched. "Why do you ask that?"

"You even go to work on weekends," I said through my clenched teeth.

"What about you? You are also busy with your beloved *children*. Reading, and reading." He stared at the wall, muttering, "Tomorrow I have an important meeting with the big boss. How about dinner? We can go out." He did not even wait for a reply and left the table.

The next night, I put on a silk dress, all made up, and waited. At midnight he showed. His excuse was that the boss took everyone at the office to dinner, and he was too busy to call. He had no recollection of his promise of the night before.

Another couple of months went by with no change. We existed as two strangers living at one address. We weren't even acting as roommates. At least, they talk once in a while. Robert stopped caring for our relationship, and I could not make him satisfied in the bedroom. His anger was brewing, and not knowing what he would do, made me anxious.

All the chemistry between the two of us was breaking down. If we were married for a long time, I could understand his behavior. As a last resort, I suggested we see a therapist to salvage this deteriorating relationship. He refused. He did not want a stranger dictating to him how to run his life. I went without him.

"Hello, Dr. Johnson." I shook hands with the therapist.

He led me into a cozy living room, very soothing and quiet. In front of the couch, a French double door opened to a beautiful lush garden, and chirping birds, a soothing scene. After taking his seat in the recliner across from me, he asked, "What is going on, Mitra?"

With a heavy heart, I responded, "My relationship is slipping away from me."

He opened his notebook and clicked his pen. "Why do you say that?"

"Robert has no interest in life with me. He only cares about his work."

"How long have you two been together?"

"Not long, a little over two years."

He wrote something, raised his head, and inquired, "Do you think he is having an affair?"

"I'm in the dark." I shrugged, "According to him, 'no'." The curious look in Dr. Johnson's eyes reminded me of my conversation with Robert when I continued, "I take his word for it. What's a relationship without trust?"

He kept quiet and moved to the edge of his seat.

After some more questions and answers, my time was up when he concluded. "The therapy will be useful if you convince Robert to join us."

He agreed to the therapy when I moved into the guest room and stopped cooking, and cleaning.

~ ❧ ~

A week later, Robert and I met at Dr. Johnson's office. He kept quiet unless the therapist pushed him. Then he grumbled, "I don't know what Mitra wants from me." Robert, in an angry voice, exclaimed, "I put a ring on her finger to get married, but she didn't want to!" While turning to me, he continued. "And now you spend most of your time reading. Why don't you cut me the slack?"

"If we have problems now," I rushed in, "why do you think it'll go away once we marry?"

After a long pause, Dr. Johnson chimed in, "Robert, would you like to respond?"

"To what?"

Dr. Johnson's bright eyes turned dull. He stared at me and said, "Mitra, would you like to see an improvement in your relationship?"

"With all my heart, but..."

Dr. Johnson cut in, "Mitra, say it to Robert," I pivoted to him, looked into his face, and said, "But when you ignore me by turning a blind eye to me," I wiped my wet eyes, "it's very demeaning and hurtful."

With lack of any emotion, Dr. Johnson responded, "What do you mean?"

I faced Dr. Johnson, "He doesn't even say hello when he comes home, and I don't even remember the last time he asked me, 'How I was?'"

The therapist started writing something in his notebook and, without raising his head, he questioned, "Mitra, what is your reaction?"

"I ignore him too! What can I do when he acts so superior?"

As if my words were hot coals thrown at him, Robert covered his face and yelled, "Not true!"

"Interesting," Dr. Johnson uttered, "Robert, would you like to tell us what's bothering you about Mitra."

Another long pause covered the room. Finally, Robert grumbled, "I don't know."

I boomed, "We barely see each other."

Dr. Johnson closed his notebook and looked at both of us, "Do you have a date night?"

I smirked and mumbled, "What is that?"

Robert winced. "It's not possible for me to plan anything." He expressed under his lips, "My work is unpredictable."

"He's right." As a bullet released from the gun, I answered, "the other night, while packing, he murmured that the next day he was leaving for San Francisco for a week." I swallowed hard. "Please tell me, didn't he have any idea about his trip a few days earlier?"

"Okay," Dr. Johnson smiled. "how would you like to have an assignment?" He stopped and turned to Robert, "Both of you being here, shows that you're committed to your relationship." Then, he revealed his remedy, "Once a week, on a Sunday afternoon, come together, sip on a glass of wine, look at your calendars, and decide which night of the week works to have a date. Is this doable for both of you?"

I nodded, but there was no reaction from Robert.

—❧❦❧—

The following Sunday around four, I called Robert to talk

about our schedule. His answer was, "I'll be there soon." At eight, he was still upstairs. I walked up and saw him hunched over a huge blueprint of a building. He raised his head, "I lost track of time. I'll be there soon."

He not only did not come down that night, but he did not ever talk with me to choose a date night. Robert exhibited no interest to save our relationship. Every day we slipped away from each other further and further.

⌐ ⌐⌐ ⌐

One last time, I visited Dr. Johnson without Robert. He concluded, "Robert has unplugged himself from you. He's baffled by how his life is going, so he hides behind his work. It's difficult to know if he would ever come around. You need to decide whether to stay or leave."

"By staying, I'll sacrifice my happiness for not being alone." I did not wait for a reply and added, "Then what about my happiness as a human being?"

With a blank face, Dr. Johnson answered, "Some women are happy to have a safety net, and that makes them satisfied in life. Decide what makes you happy."

"Then, what would be the difference between me and a slave?" I paused. "I want friendship and companionship in my life. If I wanted to be a slave or submissive, I would've abided by the fanatical regime and stayed back in my home country among my family and friends."

I thought of Harriet Tubman who rescued many slaves, and at one point she confessed that she could've saved more if they only knew they *were* slaves.

As if he read my mind, Dr. Johnson uttered, "Keep in mind once we are married, or are in a committed relationship, our feelings change. Passing time alters everything."

"For better or worse," I took a deep breath.

"Also," Dr. Johnson claimed, "Robert is resentful that you did not marry him, something he wanted, and you didn't."

I moved my head in agreement. "I can't. He is happy with me as long as I act like a puppy for him, wag my tail, and be content if he is in the mood to caress me." I sighed. "For me, this is not happiness."

"Well," Dr. Johnson said, "some of us refuse to make major decisions; instead we pout."

"Robert ruins his life and mine, by not leaving an unhappy relationship."

The therapist dismissed my remark.

In the end, I claimed, "It's obvious that I've been with Dr. Jekyll and Mr. Hyde."

"Mitra," he glanced at the clock. "Don't you think all of us at one time or another act like Jekyll and Hyde?" He then stood up.

~ ❖ ~

My life with Robert's returned to the old path. He and I were living together, but miles and miles between us. I was deep in confusion, to leave or marry and make him happy.

After a few weeks, to my surprise, he asked me to go with him to his homecoming college party at the XV Beacon Hotel, one of the most elegant hotels in Boston.

As soon as we arrived, he found the bar. Without asking me, he ordered a glass of chardonnay for me which I hate, and Johnnie Walker for himself while combing through the crowd. "Mitra, wait here, I'll be back." He walked to the other side and met one of his flames from the past, Margaret. I had seen her picture with Robert before their breakup and her marriage. Tonight, she was alone. She had to be divorced.

After I waited a while, I wandered into the hotel lobby and beyond, admiring the historic pieces of art from portraits of Presidents, to a distressed American Flag, and replicas of Venus and David. They were a pleasant reminder of what George Bernard Shaw said: *With no art, the crudeness of reality would make the world unbearable.*

I felt much better and went back to the event. Robert was on the floor with Margaret dancing cheek to cheek. As long as I could remember, after we started dating, he made it clear, "I hate dancing, and don't you ever ask me to dance."

"Then, why did you ask me to dance in Cheers?"

"I could read in your face that you're a lonely woman, and knew you wouldn't dance."

A little after dinner, Robert came to me when the crowd thinned out, "Are you ready to go?"

While driving, in his tipsy voice, he asked, "How did you like the party? Did you have a good time?"

"Not as good as you, of course," I grounded the words through my teeth.

"Don't be sarcastic." He hissed.

Back and forth, our chat turned into a heated argument. Oblivious to me, he braked so suddenly that the car screeched to a stop. He reached out, opened the door to my side, and yelled, "I've had enough of you! Get the fuck out of my car!"

In shock, I uttered, "What's the matter? Can't we get home and talk about it?"

"No! No! Right now, get out!" He came short of pushing me out.

I concentrated and averted my attention to my fancy long dress and high heel shoes, so I wouldn't trip over while climbing out his SUV. My feet barely touched the asphalt when he slammed the gas pedal. The car flew away.

After swallowing my tears, I thought about what I would do in this darkness if I get mugged. My ring was the only thing of value on me. At that moment, I realized I would be fine without it. After taking off my shoes, I pulled up my skirt, and sprinted to the opposite side of town.

In no time a car approached me from the back and scared me so much that I ran even faster until a police siren nail me to the ground. The officer stepped out, "Lady, why are you running?"

Through my tears, I explained my predicament.

Her kind voice calmed me a little. She asked, "Would you like to go home?"

I shook my head, "Please call me a cab?"

"Where to?"

I gave the address to the hotel near my house.

"Lady, do you have money in your tiny silver purse?" The other officer questioned.

I nodded. *Traveling alone, I've learned to carry my ID, a credit card, and a 20 dollar bill with me at all times if nothing else.*

The police officers waited until the cab arrived.

I stayed in the hotel for three days, and no communication between Robert and me. The clothes I changed into came from the boutique at the hotel, including my tennis shoes. I used this time to think about what I would do with my life.

On the third day, mid-morning, I arrived in front of my house. I called a locksmith. As soon as I walked in, I could not believe my eyes. Robert had cleared the house of all its furniture, including my Persian rug. He also trashed my book, and clothes all over the floor. At the first impulse, I wanted to call the police and report a robbery. The thoughts of taking him to court also flooded my mind. However, all I could do, put them in a bubble and sent them away.

Is it ever possible for the East and the West to unite in peace?

❧18❧

WHEN BABA NIMA suddenly passed on in Tehran over 7,000 miles away from me, his death shattered my world. The same was true when King Cyrus's death shattered the Persians' world. At least, Persians had Queen Atossa and King Darius to pick up the pieces for them. *But not me!* I had to grieve alone.

I was still living in Boston. For a companion, I had adopted a Maltese, Leo, six weeks old, right after my broke up with Robert. One day I received only Maman's letter, absent of Baba's. It was very much out of the norm. In every package, there was always one letter by her and one by Baba in an envelope endorsed with his handwriting. His penmanship was absolutely artistic. Not this time. With trembling hands I opened Maman's and read: *This morning when I woke up, the clock on the mantelpiece had stopped. I'm confused because I have no sense of time. Your father is in the hospital, and doctors are taking care of him. They don't know what's wrong with him.* My teary eyes prevented me to read the rest. In my family, they have always played down the severity of a situation. *Somehow I knew the worst had happened.*

Right away, I dialed their number. It was busy, busy, busy. I tried for more than a week. In those days, it was difficult to connect with Iran by phone. The war between Iran and Iraq was going on the full force since 1980. We kept hearing that America has lent a hand to Iraqis.

At last, after a week, I got through. Shockingly, I heard an operator's voice instead of Maman's.

She said, "Who are you calling?"

From her voice, I realized she had to be an Iranian operator. Without letting me say a word, she repeated, "There are no ties between Iran and America. Who are you calling?"

Through my tears, I convinced her I had to talk with my mother desperately and my father was in the hospital.

"Okay, you have only three minutes to talk." Her tone was harsh and unfriendly.

Before I could negotiate a few additional minutes, I heard Maman's somber voice: "Dear Mitra, how are you?"

"How is Baba?"

"My condolences!"

Both of us started crying. Then through her tears, she continued, "it's over forty days that Baba had passed." *Beep, Beep.*

The operator cut me off from Maman Iran.

Snail mail was our way of communication. I learned that one night a couple of months ago, Baba went to bed as usual and he was fine. At 10 AM, when he did not come out of his room, she called him. "Nima! Nima! Are you all right?" No response. She rushed to their next-door neighbor, a widow, Maryam, a few years younger than her. Both rushed back into the house. Maryam took a deep breath for courage, opened the door, and was confronted by Baba's soulless body.

I could try hard to prevent my tears running to my cheeks. The hope of seeing Baba in the future smothered me. It was as if I was on fire, and no water could subside its strength. Death, like a wildfire, destroys everything standing in its way. It had annihilated Baba, and no one, including me, could do any *damn* thing about it. *My heart burns and I can only weep.*

Moslems bury a body on the same day before sunset. For most of the Shia Iranians, there is no viewing of the dead to say their goodbyes, no fancy coffin to put an embalmed body in, to display for the family and friends. In a morgue, a washer cleanses and wraps it in a white shroud. Before they lay the body in the grave, one person from his family testifies his identity. Then, they lower the shrouded body into the tomb, and cover it with dirt until it is at the same surface as the land. *Dust to dust.*

I directed my thoughts to the ones who died during the new government. I saluted them. They were fortunate to find the ultimate freedom. I cannot believe the Iranian lives have gone into charades since Khomeini forced them into a path of fanatical religion. During the Shah's regime, we had our individuality. No harm came to us, as long as we did not verbalize *the Emperor was naked.*

Death torn Baba and me apart forever. I could not even identify his body as his eldest child, nor to be at his funeral. Suddenly, as if Baba was sitting beside me, I heard him: "Dear Mitra, when I die, do not mourn or be sorry for me. Instead, put your best clothes on and dance on my grave. My soul is freed from the prison of my body."

I cannot even do that now, no access to his grave for me.

One day, in the middle of my despair, I craved the darkness of a movie theatre. *Ghost* was my choice. Throughout the film, I had a tough time keeping up with drying my eyes. I yearned to connect with my father through a medium, the same as Molly did to communicate with her husband's spirit. Until then, I did not believe in ghosts and mediums. But Hollywood made a believer out of me. Then I started asking around until I was given an address of a British psychic. He came to my neck of the woods every other year. *So, it was my fate that this was his year to be in Boston.*

Right away, I made an appointment and went to see him. His simple room, absent of any decorations, had one recliner and a sofa. A small round table separated these two. I sat before him with a heavy heart. He never introduced himself to me. He simply asked, "Mitra, give me a personal item that you always have with you."

I looked at my bracelet.

"Yes, that would be fine."

He took it in his hand, closed his eyes, and after a few moments, he started. "Recently, you lost a man close to you. Is this correct?"

"Yes," My tears wet my cheeks. "My father!"

He went on, "I see his image in his suit and a black fedora. Your father says, 'Mitra, why are you crying? Be strong. I am happy here in a house with its rose garden.'"

Through my tears, I murmured, "Ask him, how big is the house?"

"As big as I want it to be."

"What do you do over there?"

"I read books. The ones which are not in your world yet."

"Father without you, I'm lonely."

"You need not to be. I'm always with you. Be strong! Now your mother needs you more than ever."

"When can I see you?"

"Dear, when your time comes."

It had felt like Baba Nima was sitting before me and talking with me in English. I remembered my father wore a "black fedora" in the wintertime. He read vastly and loved roses, and gardens with a pond and fountain in the middle. When we moved from Tehran downtown to the suburb, he insisted on planting a few rose bushes, two almond trees, and covered the ground with a lawn. Every spring, as soon as the garden decorated with red roses and pink blossoms, he sat beside them and read.

I had my doubts too. *How is it possible for a person to communicate with a spirit?* The psychic baffled me.

Throughout the time waiting for some closure, Hollywood and its magical world ran my life. I never knew how life was without movies and couldn't wait to forget myself in the stories depicted on the big screen. For my family, it was the only entertainment we did together. The moving pictures mesmerized us every Friday eve, whether it starred John Wayne, Sophia Loren, or Paul Newman. During the late 50s and 60s, Tehran became an extension of Hollywood. When a film premiered in America, concurrently we watched it in Tehran as well. Remarkably, America not only amused us, but also fed us Texas rice, beef, and chicken. We almost forgot how to produce rice, lamb, and chicken in our own land. Of course, the Mecca of fashions, France, was in charge of clothing us.

Baba introduced the world of illusion to me. As a teenager, he came to relish them calling himself, a "movie-holic". In his time, they had only one movie theater in Tehran, *Cinema Rex*. It showed the silent films of Buster Keaton and Charlie Chaplin. Instead of sound, a man stood close to the screen and described loudly the story to the audience. Baba spent his weekly allowance of *five rials* on buying one ticket for the first show, around 6 PM, and sat through until the usher announced the closing time around 10 or 11 PM.

"Baba, you're lucky that you were a boy." I had to get that off my chest. Despite the modernism during the Shah regime, no girl dared to walk in the street late at night without a man's escort.

He nodded, and said, "You're right, Mitra." I noticed the sorrow in his jet-black eyes. He then said, "Life in the East is much harder for women than men."

One of my best times was when Baba and I went to see *Gone with the Wind*. I was about six or seven years old. Maman was sick and throwing up, especially in the mornings. So, by the afternoon and night, she was too tired to do anything, especially sitting in a movie theatre for a long time.

That hot summer afternoon, Baba woke up from his nap, brought his shaving kit, and sat on the carpeted living room floor with his legs crossed. He placed his folded mirror in front of him on a stool. The mixture of soap with some lukewarm water in the small shaving dish smelled delicious. Then his gentle brush strokes on his face created a white mass of bubbles looked like cream-puffs. Each stuck to its place while he changed the old razor with a new one in the safety-razor shell, pulled his cheek up, and very skillfully glided the razor across his face. He also trimmed his thin mustache. He never cut himself. Before he got up, he turned to me. "Mitra, how would you like the two of us to see a movie?"

My happiness was beyond any measurement. I quickly put on my satin white dress, white mini crew socks, and shiny black shoes. Baba changed from his pajamas to a summery sport suit and tie. Right before we stepped outside, he looked at me and said, "Did you comb your hair?"

"Yes."

As if he did not hear me, he took out his black comb with tiny teeth from his inside jacket pocket and disentangled my curly short hair. He was very gentle and thoughtful not to pull even a wisp.

"Baba, we'll be late."

"Don't worry, they won't start the film until it gets dark."

In the summer, the movie theaters showed films in their huge backyards. On our way, it was impossible to ignore the envious eyes of neighborhood women in their chadors with their daughters. In the street, I saw no girl with her father.

Our first stop was at the delicatessen. The owner, Hartoon, was not born in Iran. He talked with a Russian accent. His family migrated to Iran to escape the communist party. Also, he was not Moslem either. According to Baba, in Islam, our Prophet instructed us not to eat pork because in the seventh-century hogs did not raise in a clean environment. So they carried diseases and were hazardous to human health. But not now, in our modern times.

I pulled on his jacket. "Baba, why don't we just go to the theater," I grumbled, "and get our sandwiches inside the theater?"

"They're not fresh," he breathed under his lips. "We'll buy our drinks over there."

Behind the counter, Hartoon slit the long French bread sideways. He spread mayonnaise, hot mustard, and filled it up with a few cold cuts of *kalbas*, pork meat, pickles, and pieces of tomatoes. After cutting the width of the *fat* bread into two pieces, he methodically wrapped each in a thin almost see-through piece of white paper and put them in a brown bag. He stretched his hand to me over the counter. "Young lady, would you like to carry this?"

I nodded.

On the way, I was thinking, how in the world he knew I would love to be close to the sandwiches? The smell of garlic kalbas, mixed with tiny sour pickles made my mouth watery. I could not wait to bite down into the sandwich and taste the pieces of white fat cooked inside the kalbas, and wash it down with Pepsi Cola.

I started running ahead. Outside the theater, my disappointment rose. There was a long line at the ticketing kiosk. "Daddy, why are there so many people?"

"Dear, they produce this movie for the first time in color and Cinema-Scope."

"What is Cinema-Scope?"

"It means the picture is wider and bigger than the usual. You'll see."

Baba and I were halfway through the line when a man hollered, "No more thickets!"

I tugged Baba's sleeve. "Now what are we going to do?" I felt a knot in my throat that did not go down.

All of sudden, a man in a wrinkled shirt and pants, wearing slippers, came close to us and murmured to Baba, "I have two extra tickets on the balcony, would you be interested?"

My father nodded.

"Come with me."

Both of us followed him, crossed the street, and stopped on the sidewalk. I did not hear the rest of the conversation. In the blink of an eye the man left.

My father took my hand in his when I asked, "Baba are we going home?" The misery in my voice was clear, even to me.

"No," he smiled, "let's go to see our movie."

The last sentence of the film spoken by Rhett, Clark Gable's character, stuck in my mind: "Frankly my dear, I don't give a damn." *Is that true? Men don't give a damn about women!* It baffled me. However, my father's kind eyes came to me. *He cared.* I knew.

⟨⟡ **19** ⟡⟩

1989

1989

THE DEATH OF BABA Nima left my mother by herself. Over the next several months, I determined the best way for her was to move to America and live with me or Layla. However, there was still no American embassy in Tehran to issue her a visa. The only friendly country she was allowed to travel to, was Turkey where I could meet and assist her. I kept my promise not to return to the mullahs' land. In addition, the completed covert assignment with the CIA in my background put me in direct danger the moment I would arrive.

After over two years the night before I left Boston to meet my mother in Istanbul, I made a serious mistake and watched a rerun of *Midnight Express*, made in 1968.

It's based on the true story of a young American student, Billy Hayes, who smuggled hashish from Turkey. When he is caught, he is brutalized by the Turkish guards in the prison. This film put me into sheer panic. Hollywood and its world of illusion held me spellbound. All night I had nightmares: *As soon as I arrive in Istanbul, at the airport, a few Turkish policemen attack and arrest me. They throw me in a dungeon and sexually assault me. With all my efforts, I'm still not successful to escape.* When I woke up, I was soaked in sweat.

I forgot that Billy had already committed a crime. In the "developing" countries such as Iran or Turkey, the judicial system works that a person is guilty at the time of the arrest. The defense must prove his innocence; as opposed to Western societies where a person is not guilty unless the prosecutor proves his guilt. *It's so easy to get caught in the webs of the Eastern government.*

At the Istanbul Airport, an old bus with lots of *huffs and puffs* took all the passengers to a rundown building. The uproar of a few men in wrinkled vintage jackets, worn-out shoes, and disheveled hair, separated by a high fence from us while waiting for our luggage, was like salt on my wounds.

A person from Tehran, like me, who is not from the neighboring provinces to Turkey such as Azerbaijan, does not usually speak Turkish. So I had to rely on my Farsi and English in this land of mayhem. I felt as if I'd arrived in Tehran after the revolution when our modernization and culture were demolished.

At first sight of a Turkish policeman, I thought of Billy Hayes and my nightmare. At any moment, they would attack, handcuff, and send me to a dank prison. So, I kept looking down and made no eye contact with anyone. Worse than that, I was one of a handful of women without a hijab. Those days, the Western tourists were horrified by the Islamist hijackers and did not travel in masses the way they used to.

When my tired feet on the dusty cement floor were about to give up, my suitcase appeared. During my walk through the exit tunnel, several men were shouting in Turkish. One of them stepped closer to me and in English said, "Lady, which hotel?"

My thumping heart calmed down, and I readily answered, "Hilton. Do you take American dollars?"

"Yes. Fifty dollars?"

I perceived that here, as in Iran, bargaining was a way of life. "Too much, how about twenty-five?"

"No. Hilton is far from the city."

"Then, I get a taxi."

He shrugged. "Good luck!" And walked away.

I took a few steps and stood on the sidewalk slimmer than a pencil with many people passing by. The outcry of buses, cars, omnibuses, vans, and a few wagons pulled by one or two horses from a two-way road was deafening. I had not seen any *droshky* since my childhood in Aziz's village.

All the line up of taxis were disappeared. I waited and hoped for the arrival of one. Each time, one stopped to drop off some passengers, I ran. To my surprise, the cab driver did not get out. So, the travelers took their luggage out of the opened trunk. Then he zoomed away, not enough time to get to the driver. My cough ensued as I looked around. The same driver was still leaning against the wall. He understood my predicament and walked toward me. "Lady, how about thirty-five dollars?"

Desperately, without any hesitation, I agreed.

He was nice enough to take my suitcase. In the car, all of a sudden, I remembered: I just crossed one of the forbidden lines on my list. This was not the first time I took a private car instead of a cab. My mind flew to Iran and recalled the similar experience I had when I was a professor in Tehran.

Early one evening, I left the university for the bus stop. The crowd's size and the unusual lengthy line showed the bus was delayed, or there was a cut in the number of buses for that specific line, nothing abnormal about it. The private cars began pulling to the front and whoever wanted would get in. Each car, *Paykan*, assembled in Iran, had five seats including the driver's. Every passenger accepted the price set by chauffeur before getting in. Soon an old Paykan stopped near me. By then, the car factory was shut down, and the import of any foreign cars was also forbidden. The back passenger got out when I saw a passenger in the front and one in the back. He said, "Please, go ahead."

I responded, "Why don't you sit in the middle?"

"Ma'am, I need to get out shortly."

When I sat between the two men in the back, an uneasy feeling washed over me, as the two riders were inching toward me, and their shoulders were touching mine. The driver started the engine, and his dirty jokes like freed canaries flew all over the car. The other men's laugher was an extra encouragement for him.

I took out a tissue from my purse and wiped the sweat from my forehead. Then, I called out, "Stop! Sir! Stop!"

"What's the matter, Lady?" He looked at me into his rearview mirror.

The driver's out-of-the-ordinary undertone, mixed with the grins of others, made me even more determined. Trusting my gut feeling, I shouted, "I must get out now! Stop the car!"

If he doesn't stop, I'll hit him in the head with my purse. I pushed my fingers into my purse and held it tight.

The traffic was heavy, and the driver could not speed up. He replied. "Why my Lady?"

"Please let me out!" I demanded again.

While getting out, the driver said, "This lady didn't want to have some fun."

I had to wait almost for an hour until I could get a taxi. At home, I explained everything to Maman. She hit her cheek. "Dear Mitra, thank God, you got out of the car. Since the new regime has come to power, we hear at least once a day, a woman or two, even old ones were left in an abandoned building, or in some deserted areas after being beaten and raped. It looks like women don't have security anymore."

So much for the safety of women in the Islamic Republic of Iran!

In Istanbul, if this Turkish driver kidnapped me, not a soul knew where I was. My coughing escalated. Through the window, the hustle and bustle of the city were slowly fading, and a quiet upscale neighborhood was coming into focus. I breathed easier. After almost one hour winding through some roads with smoother asphalt, the driver said, "Lady, this is the hotel."

It looked more like a mansion in the middle of the lush landscaped among exclusive houses.

"Really?" I reacted.

I had no idea how long it would take until I see Maman. Now, one year after the war, the passengers with their exit visas and tickets went to the airport every day until they became lucky to catch the flight out of Iran. However, when they couldn't get a seat, they returned the next day, and tried again.

In my room, I called Maman.

"Dear Mitra, are you in Istanbul?"

"Yes. Tomorrow go to the airport. Who is taking you?"

"Nadereh and her husband."

She was my mother's only family member, and younger than her, but married before Maman. Even generation before me, my kin did not precisely follow the tradition.

"Of course, dear. Who else?"

"They'll stay with you until you board the plane, won't they?"

"They have to," Maman's laugh was music to my ears. "In

case there's no seat for me, they'll take me back home."

"Hopefully tomorrow, you'll get a seat. Then, when they get home without you, tell them to call me collect at the hotel as of your arrival time. Do you have a pen and paper?"

"*Enshaalah,* God willing, I'll see you tomorrow midday. The flight is about three hours."

Meanwhile, I had nothing else to do and decided to take my bone-weary self to bed and have a nap until dinner. I had no idea how long I was sleeping when a booming sound and a hard jolt woke me up. At first, I thought it had to be an earthquake. I jumped out of the bed horrified, looked through the window, and saw a few men running toward the American Consulate. I rushed to the lobby. The front desk clerk read my horrified face and said, "Lady, a small bomb went off. Nothing important." With a movement of his hand, he dismissed me.

Wow! To these people, a bomb going off is not a big deal. I was shaking, swallowed my cough, and asked. "Is anyone hurt?"

"No, no, Lady, we're used to this kind of sound." He then moved away to answer the phone which was ringing off the hook.

~❧~

No news for three days, until on the fourth day my aunt's voice calmed my nerves: "Dear Mitra, your mother was successful. She boarded the plane a few minutes ago. Expect to see her soon." Then she gave me the flight information.

It was still too early to go to the airport, the 'madhouse'. Instead, I walked to the American Consulate to check it out. Its closed entrance door surprised me. There were only two soldiers bookending each side.

I approached one of them. "Excuse me, is the consulate closed?"

"Yes, because of the bomb threat three days ago. It'll be open tomorrow."

He was shocked when he heard I was there to get a visa for my mother. "For Iranians, it takes at least six months."

"Why so long?"

"But," he offered, "if you go to Ankara, the capital, at the American embassy, the waiting time is much less."

"How long there?"

"Maybe a few days."

After thanking him, I took a cab to the airport. To see Maman after all these years was a dream come true. I could not prevent my tears when I held her in my arms. So difficult to witness Baba's absence. I used to see them together all the time. *Not now, or ever.*

She hugged me. "Dear Mitra, why did you change the color of your hair?" Maman's undertone of her disapproval was clear.

"Well," I shrugged, "I mixed my dark hair of the East with the blonde hair of the West; now that I'm a mixture of both."

At the hotel, when she went to rest, I rushed downstairs to the receptionist. "Is there any flight to Ankara today?"

She turned and looked at the clock on the back wall. "No, the daily flight to Ankara is already gone."

"Is there any other way to travel there this afternoon?"

"Not really, except, the last bus leaves at 4 PM and should get you there tonight."

"How long does it take to get to Ankara?"

"It should get there by 11 PM. But buses stop along the way."

"And you really don't know exactly what time?"

Her upper lip winced. "Definitely, by tomorrow sunrise you'll be there."

I asked the lady to make a reservation at a hotel near the

American embassy. After almost an hour, she came back with a confirmation number and said, "The bus comes across the street from here. Go a little early."

Maman and I rushed to take only our handbags and left our luggage at the hotel.

At 3:30 on the dot, she and I were standing at the bus stop. At 4:30, there was no sign of the bus. A few minutes after 5:00, we saw the four-wheel drive in the distance. My mother and I were the lucky ones to get the last two seats on the bus. Mostly men, as if they have not heard: smoking is hazardous to their health. Instead of a bus, it was a moving, reeking room. It crawled through the narrow cobbled streets, alleys, green boulevards fixed up with poplar trees, palms, shrubs, and some rose bushes. The speed of the bus was slower than a turtle. But at least I could open the window and breathe a little easier. In the distance, the site of a breathtaking dome looked like hanging in the air amazed not only me but also Maman. She pointed. "Dear Mitra, what is that beautiful dome?"

"Ayasofya mosque. Hopefully, we'll have time to visit it before going back to America."

It was completely dark when we left Istanbul city-limits and the bus sped up. Around 10:00 PM, the driver announced, "One hour stop for dinner."

By this time, Maman was car sick, and my coughing would not leave me alone. She and I sat on a rock outside the cafe. Both of us welcomed an hour or so delay. When the driver called us, with loads of hesitation, we remounted the stinky bus. The next morning around 6:00 the driver pulled into the station. She and I peeled ourselves off the bus and happily got into a cab and went to our hotel.

We gobbled down some flatbread with feta cheese and washed it down with black tea. In contrast to what the receptionist in Istanbul had promised, we needed to take a taxi. We had no idea how long it took until we saw a sea of people jammed in a huge front yard overflowing into the street. Many police officers were trying to control the bovines, but they were grossly outnumbered.

"Is this really the Embassy?" I asked.

The driver pointed to a faraway, entrance gate, with the American emblem above the door. He rumbled something in Turkish. I paid him and we got out. Getting closer, I realized a line curved to the left of the building with no end. Maman and I waited at the end for our turn. After over an hour, an officer hollered, "Today, there are no more numbers for interviews! Come back tomorrow."

That can't be happening! It's only 8:30 in the morning! Though disappointed, I thought of a plan.

I pushed through the crowd, mostly Iranians. They had to be some of those people who demonstrated against the Shah, days in and days out, to bring Khomeini to power. *Now they're trying to run away.*

"Excuse me! Excuse me!" I nudged the men, women, and children to the sides, like an acrobat on a rope high up trying to keep my balance while ignoring my churning stomach. The present of Turkish police made me uneasy and sweaty. I swallowed my cough. *Do I really need to continue?* I convinced myself: I have come a long way, and could not let Maman return to Iran. *No place for her to go back.* She had sold all her belongings, and even the house. Again, I gathered my strength, and shoved through the throng. At last, I reached the entrance gate where a policeman shouted, "Where do you think you're going? Get in line with your number in your hand!"

I showed him my American passport. "Sir, I'm an American; in need of talking to my Ambassador."

For a few seconds, he stared at me with fury in his black eyes. To my amazement, he opened the gate and let me in. After passing through a manicured landscaped yard, I walked into a huge round hall. It was built like a ticket office with five kiosks. A few empty chairs were in the middle. While looking around as if I was lost in the darkness of a night, one of the gentlemen behind the glass called out, "Madam, if you're here for a visa," he pointed to my right, "on that table, there are applications, bring it back when you're done."

I picked one up. "Sir, is it possible for me to stay here and fill it out?"

"Do you have your information with you?"

"Yes, I do." *Thank God I had Maman's passport.* It took me quite some time to finish the ten-page application. When I turned in the paperwork at the only open kiosk, the clerk gave me a piece of paper. "Your interview is for tomorrow at 2:00 PM. Show this paper to the guard, so they'll let you in."

I stepped outside and encountered Maman's distressed face.

The next day, while she and I were waiting outside, we started conversing with some of the Iranians who were waiting for their visas. Most of them were stuck in Ankara for at least a year or two, hoping one day their turn would come, and they could fly to the land of the free.

I became engaged in conversation with a young Iranian girl, Jamileh. She reminded me when I was stranded in Switzerland; except, one could not possibly mistake her being French. Her hair was in a hijab, and she wore a long cotton gray jacket. A pair of black baggy pants enveloped her slim body. Full of excitement, she said, "I've been waiting here for my student visa since nine months ago.

"Why do you have to wait?"

"My area is mathematics, and I'm expecting to get the Iranian government's permission to let my family send money."

"Do you know when you'll get it?"

Jamileh shrugged. "Any day now," Then with a smirk, she grumbled, "You know how mullah's regime works. It's worse than pulling teeth."

"Meanwhile are you safe? Where do you live?"

"A rich Turkish woman rents rooms in her huge house to young, single girls. In lieu of rent, we clean her house, chicken coops, and stable."

"Does she provide you with any meals?"

Jamileh responded. "We're allowed only to cook simple dishes, rice or soup on a small burner in the stable."

In other words, the rich lady has slaves. I turned to Maman and asked, "Why do so many people leave Iran?"

"Dear Mitra," she shook her head in despair. "the situation is no good. The eight-year war between Iran and Iraq has brought the Iranian government to its knees. People don't have bread, meat, or much else to eat. Everything's rationed."

"Yes," I said disgusted, "the regime involved the people in war, so they could unite behind this extremist regime."

Then, a little girl about five ran over to me. I asked, "What is your name?"

"Ziba." She pulled her scarf closer to her eyebrows.

"Where is your mom?"

"Here she is."

A lady in chador holding an infant approached us. After greeting, Maman said, "Lady, you look tired. Come and sit with us. I'll hold your baby. I love them."

187

She gave the baby in blue swathed to Maman and sat down in front of us on the ground.

"I'm Mitra, and this is my mother, Iran."

"I'm Sakineh." She wiped her sweaty face with the corner of her chador.

She had to be hot under her black cloth covering her from head to ankles, in spite of being April. Her face was full of sorrow.

I asked, "Why did you leave Iran?"

"Oh, my lady," her voice sounded like her heart was in her throat. "Hell's better than Iran. Our country isn't as it used to be during the Shah."

"How long have you been waiting?"

"My lady, this coming fall, it will be three years." She sighed. "My family and I departed from Iran during the war," suddenly she started crying.

"Lady Sakineh, I understand." Maman said.

I was baffled.

She wiped her tears and went on, "I had a 15-year-old son, Nasir," again her tears did not let her continue.

Maman knew what she was referring to. "So sorry for losing your son."

Then, a somber silence covered our space. After a few moments, Sakineh sent some prayers to the martyrs, and uttered with a hoarse voice, "Every day, one or two Islamic police, *baseege*, went to Nasir's school and talked in each class. They encouraged the young boys to join the forces and volunteer for the front," Sakineh's heavy tears prevented her to talk further.

Maman picked up Sakineh's words as if she knew her story, "They took the boys, even 14 or 15, to the front, right then and there without even letting them say goodbye to their families."

After Sakineh ended her wailing, she said, "And urged them

that it was the best way to die. They'll be martyrs."

"And in heaven, they will be with 40 virgins," my mother finished Sakineh's thought.

The atrocities of this regime not only impact the women but also everyone including children.

Sakineh continued. "That morning, when I kissed my beloved Nasir goodbye," she wiped her tears. "I never have thought it was the last time I'd see him."

Her wailing thundered and filled the area again.

To break the sadness, I asked. "What's your baby's name?"

A smile covered her grim face. "Amir."

I replied. "Such a wonderful name for a boy. Where is your husband?"

"He is at work. That was another reason we escaped. Our mullahs were encouraging every young man, didn't matter whether single or not, also to join the Iranian force in order to defeat the Iraqis." She swallowed hard. "I encouraged him to leave. What would I've done if he were also dead?"

"Lady Sakineh," Maman said, "why don't you go back? The war has been over for a year. The country needs you, young people."

"Lady Iran, even though my husband and I are missing our homeland, to become subjects to the leader who caused my son's death,? I don't think so." She wiped her tears. "Do I want to raise this boy for the government to put him in front of a bullet again? No! No!" She pulled her chador closer to her forehead to hide her hair. "We are used to this life now. Every day I come here to hear the news from the other Iranians, and to know when we can apply for a visa to America." She then turned to Maman and asked, "When did you leave Iran?"

"A few days ago," Maman uttered.

"How is everything over there?"

"Even though the war is over, not much is changed," Maman said. "Except, now our heads and ears take a break from the Iraqis' planes bombing our cities, including Tehran."

As if Nasir was far from her mind, Sakineh asked. "Do people have enough to eat?"

The baby started to cry. Maman returned him to Sakineh and said. "Well, not much better than the time of the war. If you have money, and I mean being super-duper rich, you can buy everything in the free market. However, the rest of us rely only on coupons issued by the government. And based on the numbers of each family, they're allowed to get only that much every month."

Sakineh confirmed with a nod. "I remember, everyday, before dawn, I went and waited in line until noon or later to get some items to cook one time meal for that day." She kissed the baby, and started breast-feeding him.

How come, a woman' hair rises a man's sexual fantasy, but not her breast?

With a calm face, Sakineh continued, "See, I lived in a farm in Azerbaijan." She claimed, "Even though we were self-sufficient, we could keep nothing. Everything had to be sent to the front."

I pretended to defend the government. "But, Khomeini, as a supreme leader, had no choice. Iraqi forces attacked Iran first."

"Lady Mitra," Sakineh said, "the Shah kept us strong and Saddam Hossain didn't dare to attack us."

"Military strength, not headstrong," I uttered.

She was right. When I was 13, during a televised ceremony, the dashing Shah in his military uniform with a broad chest full of colorful medals welcomed the latest addition to the Iranian Air Force: an American F-14 Fighter Jet, a brand new innovation of America. He announced, "Now, our sophisticated military is equal to America. We walk shoulder to shoulder with the United States. We have secured our superb strength in the world."

How come he was so wrong?

I was proud of these immigrants who left their homeland to chase their dreams for the sake of their children. I was however baffled. The majority of these people had demonstrated against the Shah. The women covered themselves under their black chador, screamed, and cried out for an Islamic Iran until Khomeini arrived in Tehran from Paris. He for sure changed the face of Iran and took its people back even before the seventh century when no one specifically women, had any rights. I wished at least he would've taken the Iranians to the time of our Prophet Mohammad when he brought us Islam, a civilized religion. *Khomeini can't even keep the people satisfied, even the ones who supported him.*

"Lady Sakineh," I asked. "did you participate in demonstrations against the Shah?"

She nodded and looked at the ground.

"Then, why?"

"Dear Lady, we made a mistake." She breathed a deep sigh. "Our mullahs filled our ears with the nonsense that the Shah isn't a devout Moslem but rather a corrupted leader."

"And if that was not enough," Maman interrupted Sakineh's words, "some groups threw a cassette tape with the Khomeini's speeches into every house."

"Yes, yes," Sakineh affirmed. "I got several of them. Whether it was his voice or not, we don't know. But words of bad-mouthing the Shah were heard everywhere."

The line between Maman's eyebrows became deeper. "It all started with the Cinema Rex fire in downtown Tehran."

"Yes, such a tragedy," I exclaimed. "the Shah blamed it on the Moslem terrorists."

Sakineh's voice became angry. "But not according to the cassettes we received."

"She is right." Maman turned to me. "Pro Khomeini group, when the movie theatre was full, in the middle of the film, the Savak personnel locked the exit doors and started the fire. No one could run out, and near to 100 people died."

Sakineh and Maman sent prayers to the dead.

Then Maman uttered, "We don't know who to blame, the Shah's Savak, or the Khomeini's followers? But, now the people must suffer for supporting a bunch of uneducated mullahs who don't have any clue how to run a country."

Wow! The Shah of Iran had three strikes against him: First, the allies brought him to power by sending his father to exile. Second, in 1953 with a help of the CIA, he regained the crown. However, he could not survive the third one, the uprising of the religious extremists.

My thoughts were interrupted when I heard Maman's name from the loudspeaker. She and I wished Sakineh and her family the best of luck and rushed inside. During the interview, while we were standing at the kiosk, I explained to the clerk, "Sir, I'm my mother's translator. May I accompany her?"

"Sure! Sure!"

He then looked at the paperwork, raised his head, and in a kind word uttered, "I see, you're applying for a visa on her behalf. What do you do?"

He was amazed when he found out that I also studied at UCLA as he did. After chatting about his interesting memories from his days in school, he said, "I don't see any problem with your mother's visa. But, before finishing up, there is a form you must sign."

"What form? Wasn't the paperwork complete?"

"Yes, yes." Then he put a piece of paper in front of me. "By signing this, you are promising that once you take her, you won't apply for her permanent residency."

"Sir, you know well it's my right as an American to ask for her residency."

He whispered, "I can't tell you what to do when you get to the United States. Without your signature, no visa can be issued for her."

If I had to give my life for the price of taking Maman with me to America, I would've done so. After I signed the form, he said, "Come tomorrow before noon to get her visa."

Maman was baffled. "What happened?"

I turned to her with a smile. "Let's go."

She followed me outside.

We had to return to Istanbul because of our luggage. No way was I going back inside another "moving chimney". We could make a reservation to fly back.

The next day, after getting her visa, we went directly to the airport. A little over an hour, we landed in Istanbul.

Pan Am had no flight until the following day at noon. I made a reservation for both of us, and we took a cab to the Hagia Sophia, Holy Grand mosque. To my surprise, the caretaker was neither dressed as a priest, nor as a mullah. He even let Maman and I go inside without a hijab. In Iran, even during the Shah's regime, any woman attending a mosque had to hide behind our traditional cloth, chador.

Inside was a feast to our eyes. The vast hall made us believe we'd stepped into a majestic land. Originally, it was built as a church, then, a mosque. The Cathedral's walls were decorated with calligraphy in *Allah, Mohammad, and Ali,* written or etched in black or white marble. In between them the sculptures of Mother Mary holding Jesus as a toddler, or the images of Christ depicted the togetherness of these two religions. This mosque truly had brought Christianity, and Islam together in harmony. *Unbelievable!* In the country where its rulers built such a divine place to show us glimpses of Heaven, they could also have brutality as depicted in *Midnight Express.* I admitted sadly, we as modern humans, like sheep, are easily influenced by the world of illusion as if we are in a deep sleep. We eagerly solve our differences with each other with guns and violence. For sure, we have turned a deaf ear to our prophets' instructions. As if Mohammad, Christ, Moses, Buddha, and all other religious leaders never illuminated the path of love and harmony for us.

The following day, while it was still dark, we checked out of the hotel, and a taxi dropped us off by the airport. A couple of Turkish police officers stood menacingly by the entrance door. One of them asked for Maman's passport. After he looked through all the pages, he started saying something in Turkish.

I rushed up and in English said, "Sir, is there a problem?"

In an angry voice, he yelled, "The plane has a stop in Zurich. As an Iranian citizen, she must have a Swiss visa too." He then closed the passport and shoved it into her hand.

"But why?" I pleaded.

"Likely, in New York, they won't let her in the country. Then she'll be deported here."

"But why not to Iran, her home country?"

"Lady, where did you come from? There is no flight between America and Iran."

"Yes, sir, you're right." In a friendly tone, I tried to negotiate, but with a Turkish officer, no way. I said, "What can she do?"

"She must get a Swiss visa too."

There was no time for me to get disappointed, or argue with him. It was too early to go to the Swiss Consulate, so, we took a taxi back to the hotel, checked in again, left our luggage there, and set out to pursue yet another visa for Maman.

A taxi let us out in front of the Swiss consulate. I didn't know whether it was my dire face or my mother's weeping that right away the receptionist called the consul. He invited us to his office, and in a friendly voice asked. "Have a seat, please! What is the problem?"

After he heard our predicament, he responded, "Your mother doesn't need a Swiss visa." His calm voice washed away my anger. "Pan Am's representative takes responsibility for the foreign passengers. Besides, in Zurich, no passenger gets off the plane. Who told you she needs a Swiss visa."

"A Turkish officer at the airport."

"Right now, go to the Pan Am airline office." He looked up the address on his Rolodex, jotted it down, and gave it to me. "They'll make a reservation for you both, and put a code on her passport that the Turkish officers allow her to board."

When we reached Pan Am airlines, both of us wished that this would be our last stop. The office was quiet. It seemed as if it were a long way from the Turkey. A very polite middle-aged Turkish man took our tickets and her passport. After a few minutes, he came back, "You two are all set for tomorrow's flight."

"So," I said cautiously, "my mother doesn't need a Swiss visa?"

"No, not at all." He showed me the seal in her passport, "This blue seal, 52A, shows that PanAm returns any passenger who is refused the entry to the U.S." He handed it to Maman, and with a smile said, "Have a pleasant flight."

The next day, when we arrived at the airport again, police officers were pushing and shoving the people to stay in line. When the officer kindly guided Maman to wait in a line to clear customs, my churning stomach calmed down. In the middle of mayhem, while waiting, I noticed the two different lanes, on the right for Americans or Europeans, and the other for Turkish and other citizens. The officers did not open the suitcases of the Westerners. But on the left they threw out almost all of the items in a suitcase as if they were looking for *hashish*. So, I hastily changed my small suitcase with Maman's two huge ones.

I reached the other side in a heartbeat, but not Maman. Her turn came up after quite some time. As the officer opened the suitcase, his eyebrow flinched. I started trembling and my cough started harshly. My thought was: *For sure, he'll recognize that the slim skirts, blouses, and couple of blue jeans pants do not belong to this hefty woman covered in hijab. Any moment, the Turkish officers will attack me for my dishonest act.*

But luck was on our side that day. The officer closed the suitcase, gave it to her, and signaled the next passenger. I took a deep breath and smiled in triumph.

On the plane, after about half an hour, the pilot announced, "We're cleared for takeoff."

I clapped and breathed much easier.

Unfortunately, Maman Iran lived for a short time with me. She became terminally ill and followed Baba Nima to heaven.

20

IN THE SPRING, Tucson, like a kaleidoscope, attracts throngs from all over the world. The Sonoran Desert comes to life with many rainbow-colored blooms. The variety of cactuses, rows of wildflowers including forsythia, snowy winter-jasmine, and cosmos in every shade, would put the astonishing paintings of Monet or Matisse to shame.

The calling of the mountains had been impossible to ignore. Wasson Peak reminds me very much of Damavand Peak in Tehran. Here, the natural beauty had awakened me. Like Rip Van Winkle, after a long sleep. *I feel though I'm part of the lost generation.*

Three years ago I moved to this sleepy town with my aged dog, Leo. Maman was deceased, and my younger sister, Layla, and her Persian husband had moved to Tehran. The Iranian government had invited all its citizens living abroad, especially in America to return and help in building a new Iran.

My beloved Leo was slowing down. He had given me unconditional love throughout the years. His racing heart against my chest was for sure a sign of losing his grip on life. His big black eyes were full of gratitude. He had been surviving despite his breathing problem. I loved him like the baby I never had. I swallowed my tears and rejected the thoughts of my future without him. Then, I reflected on Rilke's saying, *Let everything happen to you; Beauty and terror. Just keep going. No feeling is final.*

I glanced at the clock. In an hour, Rosemary would be here to pick me up to attend Ganji's gathering. She was my friend from the Tucson Chamber of Commerce. The anticipation of seeing her cheerful face and pear-shaped body brought a smile to me. Several times she had encouraged me to go with her: "Mitra, you've got to hear him. He is so different from other gurus."

"Does he instruct us to meditate?"

"Not meditation per se. Besides, what is wrong with meditation?"

"Absolutely nothing." I thought about it and explained, "Except, whenever I meditate for a few minutes, I feel like I'm under water and can't breathe. So I open my eyes."

Rosemary looked at me as if she was observing a creature from Mars.

Throughout my life, I was well aware, that there was no harmony between my body and soul, as if an invisible *steel curtain* divided me into two halves. I had hope Ganji would bring down this unseen curtain and make me whole. As a modern woman, I confess: During the years, I have denied my soul and concentrated on only the materialistic world, and lived in *illusion. I must give this a try.*

In my arms, Leo's breathing returned to normal. I put him in his bed and started to get ready.

Rosemary parked by a steep hill and pointed out, "We have to walk up this little hill to Ganji's home."

"This is more like a mountain than a hill," I laughed.

She took a deep breath. "Ganji comes here for only four months out of the year."

"Then he is a 'snowbird.'" I was proud to know the Arizonians' term for the crowd coming to Tucson during the winter fleeing cold climates.

Rosemary turned to me. "He stays with this couple, the owners of the house."

"Are they his family?"

"I don't know, but definitely they're ardent followers."

"Is his fee as steep as this *hill?*"

With a smile, Rosemary responded. "Only donations, he believes he doesn't need very much to live on."

"*I respect those who can live simply.*" *I moved my head up and down.* "I wish it was possible for me to do so."

Rosemary panted heavily. "I guess, materialistic world has corrupted most of us."

After a few minutes, we reached the flat land surrounded by bushes of white roses.

"Ganji, his name sounds Indian," I pointed out. "Where is he from?"

"Actually, his ethnicity is a mystery," Rosemary replied. "He says, 'I'm from the human race.'"

We proceeded to the adobe hut at the far right edge of the land.

Upon our arrival, we took off our shoes and left them with the other pairs at the entrance door. Inside, in a small living room, three other women and one man were sitting on the floor in a circle. When Rosemary and I had taken our seats on the furnished cushions, they all introduced themselves. The lady with silver hair looked like the oldest was Charlotte. Emily's red hair gathered like a bird's nest on top of her head. She appeared to be in her 30s. Sonia's curly, dark hair framed her fleshy face.

She looked about forty. Mark looked a little older than us but not as old as Charlotte. He had pulled his long hair in the back. His washed-off denim shirt and jeans were signs of his adherence to hippies' time. His twinkling eyes showed his interest in learning something in the arena of spirituality.

Soon, Ganji entered the room. His look made me feel certain that he was from somewhere in the Eastern hemisphere. A white cotton cloak and black pants covered his tall stature and boney body. His shoulder-length salt and pepper hair was a reminder of Dervishes. I recalled. *The gag rule on the Persian Dervishes was a tragedy in Iran. It kept their message of Love and Freedom in darkness. If it weren't for Emerson and other Western thinkers who spread the Eastern philosophy, no one would've known about the mysticism of the East, or Sufism.*

"Good afternoon," Ganji uttered in a peaceful voice, then settled into the last seat, making the circle complete. "Welcome everyone. Please keep in mind, I will not preach. I believe in what Socrates said: 'I cannot teach anyone anything, I can only make them think.'"

I felt at peace. *He won't dictate to us that his way is the only and the right way.* I eagerly focused on his words.

"I can tell, each one of you is an accomplished individual. But are you happy? Regardless of what life dumps on you, do you feel joy within?"

We all shook our heads left and right.

"If you are here," Ganji articulated, "you must be searching for an answer in your life."

Charlotte raised her hand and said, "I want to be free of shame. It stops me from being happy."

I got a boost of confidence and followed her, "I think there's a steel curtain separating my body and soul. What can I do to connect them?"

Emily volunteered, "My problem is, not having enough money."

"Not enough love," Rosemary spoke up.

My mind grappled with the word 'love'. *What does love mean exactly?*

Ganji's warm voice drew everyone's attention back to him. "And you all are here looking to me to fix everything for you?" He grinned.

"Why is it so difficult?" Without a fear, I opened my heart. "As a modern woman, not to feel a harmony in my body and soul like my ancestors?"

Rosemary jumped in, "Do you think people in the past were much happier?"

The rest affirmed with nodding when I exclaimed, "As far as I know, the savior of the Zoroastrian religion, Reverend Mitra, and other Persian women or even men in ancient times confronted many more volatile situations than we do." I stopped to think for a moment. Then I continued. "their tasks in life made them satisfied; whether to serve as a priest, soldier, governor, or teacher. The secret of balancing their materialistic and spiritual world was quite clear to them."

While nodding, Ganji said, "Absolutely. Every individual's attention was on creating harmony within him or herself. To do so, they happily serve the society."

"Not like the modern human who tends to be fragmented," Mark announced.

Ganji's enthusiastic voice blanketed the room, "Why do you think it was so?" He paused; then when the silence continued, he went on, "In the past, as human beings, most Easterners worked on their two sides, body and soul, to make themselves complete."

After a moment, I asked, "Is that because they had a strong faith in their religion?"

"That's one way to look at it," Ganji concurred. "Those people had an anchor. It was their religion."

Mark interjected, "That was the East. The West didn't have religion."

"The West had philosophy," I voiced.

"She's right." Sonia, sitting on my right broke her silence. "When Alexander conquered Persia, he wanted to blend the two worlds. But eventually, his soldiers rebelled against him and forced him to return to Greece."

"And Persians," I finished her thought, "kept their religion and brought back their kings."

"Okay," Ganji took over, "what would happen if a boat has no anchor?"

His obvious question caused us to laugh. Ganji continued, "What can be an anchor for a person?"

"Money? When a person is rich, he is happy and powerful," Mark declared.

"Knowledge," Charlotte attested.

"How about thinking of the past?" Rosemary questioned.

Emily smiled, "Especially of the good old times."

Ganji with a subtle grin, responded, "How long do you think these anchors will last?"

"In my culture," I asserted, "to think of the past is the anchor for most of us." I paused. "We even talk about it for hours, no present or future exists for most of us. Whatever happens, is Allah's will."

"True, true," Ganji exclaimed. "Most Easterners concentrate only on the past, and most Westerners plan for their future."

"That's not totally true," Mark stated. "Here, we think of the present and future, and easily forget the past."

"Let's talk about 'time' differently," Ganji suggested.

"Is there another way?" Sonia asked surprised. "We always

imagine 'time' as a horizontal line starting from birth and ending with death."

Ganji looked at her and went on, "How about if we teach our minds," he took a short pause, "to only think in the present, and have a vertical line. It goes only up and up in the present." He stopped to study each one's face.

"Mr. Ganji," Charlotte eagerly uttered, "you sound like Shakespeare."

I finished her statement, "The world is a stage, and we're all playing our parts."

"Yes, life happens only in the present time." We concentrated on Ganji's words. "I'm sure you've heard that some African tribes don't have any past or future tense in their language. Therefore, they exist only in the present."

I asked, "Does that mean to be mindful?"

Ganji nodded. "Mindful and conscious."

"To honor the past, be present," Charlotte offered.

Mark held his head in both hands and blurted out, "It's impossible, no way. Our train of thoughts goes all over, especially when we are alone."

"Yes, for sure," Ganji confirmed. "Let me ask. Do you inhale and exhale?"

We all burst out laughing.

Ganji continued, "Do you do that in the past, present, or future?"

Our cheery murmurs enveloped the room when Ganji yet again threw another question at us. "What is the most positive emotion we have?"

I responded gaily, "Love, of course."

"Exactly!" Ganji had another question: "What is the opposite of love?"

"Hate." I did not give a chance to anyone else.

"Perfect. What happens during our inhales and exhales?"

"All of us know that," Mark said.

"Tell us, please," Rosemary implored.

Emily chuckled. "We inhale oxygen and exhale carbon dioxide."

"One feeds us good stuff," I added, "and the other gets rid of *poison* in us."

Ganji, like a bandleader teaching us one note at a time, explained how to do the exercise. "So, when we inhale, with your inner voice pronounce the word, *love*. Then, at the time of exhaling, utter, *hate,* or any word you want to substitute for it." He stared at us one by one. "Let's practice. Sit up straight, if you feel more comfortable, close your eyes. Ready? Inhale, *love*. Exhale, *hate*. Again, inhale, *happiness*. Exhale, *sadness*. Again, inhale, *love*. Exhale, *judgment*. Inhale, *Light*. Exhale, *darkness*. Do this breathing technique on and off for several days and see the difference in your mood and well-being."

In awe, I said, "In this way, we concentrate inward rather than outward."

Ganji clapped once in affirmation.

Mark frowned. "What is the purpose?"

Ganji kindly replied, "The meeting of *inner* and *outer*."

"But, what if we forget?" Rosemary asked. "Too busy making a living to remember."

Ganji turned to her. "Practice, practice, and practice. You need to learn to love your inner self, not your sensual *self*. In other words, breathe in *love*, and breathe out *hate*, or any negative words which come to your mind; this makes you conscious of your inner world."

I smiled inwardly. *Now I know the secret of Reverend Mitra. She only practiced Good Thoughts which produced Good Words and led to Good Deeds. No wonder she was strong enough to face the upheavals of life without being destroyed by them.*

Later that night, for the first time in a long time, I lay down, blanketing myself in peace, while repeating Ganji's last words: "Keep in mind, unless we change inwardly, our world will not change."

Now I know the right place to find real love, within my Self.

‿❀21❀‿

2005

IN MY HEART, Ganji has left an everlasting footprint. I have been practicing at least once a day: inhale, *love* and exhale, *hate*. The anchor of love prevents my mind from being stranded in the stormy sea of life. Lately, mentally and physically, I feel stronger, no need to wear soozany over my shoulders. Amazingly, there was no return of my coughs either.

In Tucson, I feel satisfied. As a literary agent working remotely with an agency in New York, I kept quite busy. To stay in the present illuminates my life. I realize one cannot love and react to the outside world properly when she doesn't know herself inwardly. *I'm a complete woman rejoicing my being.*

My poor dog, Leo's difficulty with breathing, breaks my heart. I used to see unconditional love in his huge black eyes, but no more. They look like two tired dots sitting on his white face. He has no appetite, and at least once a day he has a convulsion. Dr. Brown has been his regular veterinarian. A year ago, she said, "All these medications are just keeping Leo comfortable," She stared into my eyes, "since you don't want to put him through surgery to fix his collapsed trachea."

"He's almost fifteen years old, and I don't wish him to suffer any longer," I responded through my tears.

"Keep in mind, there will be a time when the medications don't work any more, and you'll need to decide." Dr. Brown stopped when she saw my uncontrollable tears running down my cheeks.

Is it right for us to lengthen life of our loved ones for our own happiness?

To forget about letting Leo go, I concentrated on the present. These days, technology has taken a quantum leap. Everyone talks about the latest innovation, Facebook.

I have been separated from my friends and family members for several years. Like most Iranians, we scattered all over the world. Perhaps, with Facebook, I will be able to find them. My determination to sign up got the better of me, and at last, I posted my profile.

A few months later, I found and connected with Bahar, my friend from high school. She married the love of her life right after graduating from high school. She and her family have lived in Germany for a few years. We can travel to either country and see each other, such a joy it would be.

Another day, I received a "friend request" from John Davis. It was easy to recognize him. I never forgot his baby blue eyes and blond hair. Even back then I knew I was a sucker for the Western look. *Wow!* After over 35 years, I have pinpointed this precious friend. My delight was out of control when I accepted his friend request.

After Leo started fainting several times a day, I decided it was time to let him go, a tough decision. I searched and searched for a way to brace myself. I had to choose between keeping Leo or letting him go. It would be much easier if it were me. This tongue-tied creature could not even say, 'yeh' or 'nay'. *I feel like a murderer.*

After a few days, with a heavy heart, I opened the door to Dr. Brown. "Dear Mitra," she sighed. While I was petting Leo, she continued, "He's suffering, and you're giving him freedom from continuous pain."

I exhaled through my tears. Then, Dr. Brown instructed me to hold him on my lap while she injected him with a sedation drug, and after a few minutes another drug, releasing Leo from the prison of his ravaged body. *You're free, my dear. Free at last.* I wished when my time comes, instead of letting me suffer in order to lengthen my physical life, I would have the choice of freedom sooner than later.

My thoughts were with John while driving to the airport. After several months communicating on line and many phone calls, he is coming for a weekend visit. At Tucson International Airport, unlike LAX, or JFK, to find a parking place is easy, no sign of any hustle and bustle, even though it was a Friday evening. To soothe my nerves, I walked around the terminal. After reading on the monitor that his flight had landed, I went in through the huge double glass door to the gate, trying to ignore my thumping heart. As I combed through the passengers trickling out, my eyes ceased on a bald man, no longer young. *Is that John? Without his blond hair?* The stranger stared back into my face with his sharp blue eyes.

Both of us smiling, he said, "Mitra? Is that you?"

"Yes," I responded eagerly.

Our laughter filled the arrival space, and our hug lasted long. Neither one of us wanted to let go of the other as if we were making up for the bygone years.

To reunite with a long-lost friend has made me joyful. "John, I never thought one day I would see you again."

"Neither did I." He embraced me again earnestly. "I thought you had plans to return to Iran after your education."

"I did. It's a long story."

"Do you live here in Tucson now?"

"Yes, for good."

In the car, I said, "I'm happy to find you. I never could forget how nice you were to me when my car broke down."

"That's what friends are for."

"For dinner, I made a reservation at Vivace, a fancy Italian restaurant. I hope you like Italian food, as much as I do."

"Love it."

During our cocktails, he asked, "Mitra, what do you usually do for a weekend?"

"Tomorrow, being Saturday, I go jogging and read. At night I have a season ticket for the Rouge Theater. If you're interested, I'll get you a ticket. If not, we can do whatever you would like."

"What is the play?"

"Waiting for Godot,"

John smiled.

"What is your smile for?"

"My first year at the University of Chicago, I took a theater course. I played Vladimir in *Godot*."

"Wow, so you must like the theater of the absurd?"

"Of course. And I'm interested to see how it's done on the stage in modern time." He held my hand in his, "Let's find out if I can get a ticket." He took a sip of his Martini. "Let's not forget for the sake of the good old days, one night we need to

go dancing, too. So, I can teach you how to disco all over again."
He burst out laughing.

"Seriously?" Then I tried to think. "I don't know anywhere in Tucson to go dancing." I paused. *Should I take a chance? Why not!* "I guess, that needs to be when I come to Chicago."

His eyes lit up. "Will you come to Chicago?"

"I'd love to."

"When?"

"Soon, if that's okay with you."

He grinned. "More than okay."

I picked up an olive from the Antipasta dish and casually asked, "What is your status now?"

"Last time," he paused.

"You were taken."

"Not now!" He put his hand on mine. "My wife and I are divorced for a long time."

"Any serious girlfriend?"

"Too busy working, no time for a girlfriend."

"How come?"

"My two children's education expenses: Beth, twenty-three, is in medical school, and Keven, twenty, just started law school."

I raised an eyebrow. "He wants to become a hot-shot lawyer like his daddy."

John shrugged. "And I don't know why?"

The butterflies in my stomach were hard to tame. This man made me realize that in my heart, I always loved him, as a dear friend. But is it possible we can now be more than just friends?

During his three-day visit, I became confident that I had found the missing link in my life. For me, it was not important to marry him or not. The most important point in my life was, he understands me. We always had plenty of subjects to talk about for hours; over art, philosophy, psychology, and even politics despite our different points of view. We could enjoy each other's company and friendship. *All I've been dreaming about in my ideal man.*

On the final night, he wrapped his arms around me and hugged me like he never wanted to let me go. He whispered in my ear, " Mitra, I think I'm falling in love with you."

I loved the way he kissed me. When his full-bodied lips came in contact with mine, they felt soft and moist, without trying to win a battle, but seeking union and closeness to share my breath. Then, I rested my head against him and began crying tears of joy. "I can't believe, after all these years, we found each other," I murmured into his chest.

I saw in myself that I was falling in love with him as well.

On the way back home from dropping John off at the airport, I felt I had developed a strong heart. I owe all of it to Reverend Mitra whose wisdom guided me to recognize and understand how to live in harmony. Amazingly, I do not feel alone or lost in life anymore. *I am a completely modern woman. Inhale, love. Exhale, loneliness.*

Now I can read the signs and make the right decisions, to be the person I want to be in control of my life. Where once life controlled me like a leaf in the wind; *now, I am the wind.*

AUTHOR BIO

As a biographer, storyteller, and author, Nooshie Motaref has written *Bird of Passage*, a sequel to the Award-winning novel, *Tapestries of the Heart*, and *Land of Roses and Nightingales*.

She has gone through many challenging life experiences, unlike many women from the Middle East. Nooshie grew up in Persia, and studied in four countries — Iran, Germany, Switzerland and United States. She received her master's and doctorate degrees in American Literature and Folklore from Florida State University. Her dissertation is a proof of Carl Jung's theory, the "Collective Unconscious," through Persian fairytales and folktales.

In March 2014, she presented one of her articles, "Women and Islam," for a conference, Women and Education at Oxford University in Oxford, England. She gives speeches on several subjects related to her birthplace, including its culture, traditions and religion. Her purpose is to familiarize Western audiences with Iranian life and ethnicity.

Six years ago, Nooshie moved to Tucson to be near her son and his family, including her young grandson. She remains active in local non-profit organizations. *Tucson Tellers of Tales* (TOT), a national storytelling organization; she was president from 2019 to 2020, and now she serves as the treasurer. She is also a member of the CV chapter at the *Philanthropic Education Organization* (P.E.O.) where women help women reach the stars. The other organizations are: The American Association of University Women (AAUW), and Facilitator's Guild, by Center for Community Dialogue and Training.

Please visit www.nooshiemotaref.com

CPSIA information can be obtained
at www.ICGtesting.com
Printed in the USA
LVHW042342310122
709930LV00003B/60